Over You

by

Nona Day

SOUL Publications

Nona Day   Over You

SOUL Publications

Jarvis

J stood in front of the wedding hall with my brother in law, Dak beside me as my best man. Of course my business partner, Noble and Brandon, who was like a little brother to me stood beside me. After Brandon's mom died, my parents made sure him, and his father was straight since his dad and mom were close friends with my parents. After my parents' death, I stepped in to do what I knew my father would do and that's make sure Brandon and his father never went without. We weren't blood, but I loved him no less. I also had my childhood friend, Axel as a groomsmen. He ran the streets with me when I first started. He remained solid and came up in the game with me. Two of my fiancée's brothers stood beside me for my wedding day. To be honest, I couldn't remember the names of any of the bridesmaids. All I knew was I fucked a couple of them and had them sign a non-disclosure agreement. On this day, I was supposed to be filled with love and thoughts of living the rest of my life with Valentine. She was the perfect woman:

beautiful, classy, goal-oriented, submissive and claimed to love me, but I knew she didn't. Everything about her was a man's dream. Any man would've been lucky to have her as his wife, but I wasn't that man. I doubted if there was a woman on earth that could make me love her so deeply that I wanted her to know my soul. Well, there was one, but I fought every single damn day to push her disloyal, weird ass to the back of my head. Blood started to rush to my head just thinking about her. The rising rage started to cause my ears to ring. Mixed with the annoying chatter in the wedding hall, I was on the verge of losing it. Only thoughts of her could bring me to this point. My ears zoned in on the not-so-low whispers coming from Amoy and Cache seated on the front row of the groom's side.

"I think he's actually going to do it," Cache said. I glanced at Amoy and she rolled her eyes at me and crossed her legs. She hated that I was marrying Valentine. It's not that she didn't like her, but she felt I didn't love Valentine enough to marry her. I knew I didn't love her at all, but I was determined to do this.

"He's not going to do it. Look at him. He's about to blow a damn fuse just thinking about committing to and trusting someone," Amoy replied to Cache. I had no plans of trusting anybody with my heart. Valentine damn sure wasn't getting my soul. I would provide for her as a husband does for his spouse, but I wasn't with all that love shit. Valentine knew that and didn't care. She claimed she loved me, but I knew she only loved what I could offer. It was my power and ambition that made her heart love me. With a pre-nup signed, I was willing to give it a shot.

"I don't know, Amoy. He looks like he's determined to marry her," Cache said.

"He's not going to marry her. I'll bet you," Amoy replied adamantly.

"Two hundred dollars," Cache said. Amoy agreed to the bet and they shook hands on it.

"Girl, look at my damn husband. He's looking fine as hell in that tux. I'm doing Simone Biles gymnastic on that dick tonight, and he's going swimming in this pussy like Michael Phelps," Cache said. Amoy laughed louder than she intended. She immediately covered her mouth to muffle her laughs.

"Sssshhh!" I said looking over at them. Cache licked her tongue at me in a childish manner.

SOUL Publications

"I'm going to throw your wives out my wedding if they don't be quiet," I said glancing at Dak and Noble.

"Nigga, you supposed to be happy right now. You acting like a nigga getting ready to walk down death row," Dak said.

Before I could reply the music started playing. Everyone stood up waiting for Valentine to make her entrance. The hall doors opened, and she stood there looking like a picture of perfection. It felt like an eternity had passed before her father finally walked her to me. I shook his hand before he placed Valentine's hand in mine. I could hear the pastor talking but I wasn't listening to anything he had to say. We had rehearsed this wedding day so many times I could've been the pastor and the groom at the same time. I knew his speech word for word.

I stared at Valentine as he spoke. She truly was picture perfect with her russet skin, slanted eyes, high cheek bones, snub nose, and sexy, plump lips. Her natural beauty never required any makeup, but she had enough layers on to supply a funeral home for a year. Nothing was out of place on her. Not even a strand of hair. *Stop it!* I screamed the words in my head because I could never stop comparing everyone to Nova. She could never look this perfect and that was one of the things I liked most about her.

Nova was the complete opposite of Valentine in every way possible. Nova was messy and goofy with no ambition. She hated the power that money held over people, but Valentine loved it. With all those negatives, she still held an energy that drew me in and had some kind of mystical lock on my mind. She was just as beautiful as Valentine with her umber skin, Nubian nose, high cheek bones, and full, luscious lips. Valentine always wore her hair bone straight. Nova's hair was a wild curly mess every day. I wanted to marry someone that would never make me think of her. But here I was thinking of her on my wedding day.

I was pulled from my thoughts with a nudge from Dak. Looking at him to see what the problem was, he nodded at the pastor.

"Do you?" The pastor asked.

"Do I what?" I asked irritated, still thinking of Nova. I heard Amoy and Cache giggle. I gave them a stern look and they cut it off immediately.

"Do you take Valentine Shanice Durden to be your lawfully wedded wife?" The pastor repeated his question. I stared at Valentine. She held a loving, pretty smile showing her pearly white teeth waiting for my confirmation to have her as my wife.

"Oh yea, I mean no," I answered quickly. "Wait, what was the question again?"

God spared me when Dak collapsed on the floor. Amoy jumped up and rushed to him screaming his name. I kneeled down beside Dak and demanded everyone give him room to breathe. Amoy was crying and trying to wake him up. I could hear Valentine calling my name, but I ignored her.

"Cache, please calm her down so we can see what's wrong with him," Noble told her. Cache pulled Amoy away from Dak's unconscious body. The minute she was out of sight, Dak opened his eyes and winked at me before closing them again. I was relieved to know he was okay and thankful he came to my rescue.

"Let's get him in a car. He needs to get to a hospital," I said to everyone.

"I'm a doctor!" Someone yelled. *Damn!* I needed to get as far away from this wedding as possible. Valentine was standing behind me begging me to say "I do" so we could be pronounced man and wife. I completely ignored her.

"Nah, he needs to see his specialist," Brandon lied.

"What? What specialist? Oh my God! How long has he been sick? What's wrong with him?" Amoy asked frantically.

"Help me get him to a car," I said.

All my groomsmen helped me carry Dak out of the hall like he was really unconscious. The limo was parked in front of the building, so we put Dak inside. Noble and I got in with him. Before I could close the door, Amoy and Cache jumped in with us. The moment the limo doors were closed, Dak sat up. Amoy stared at him with tears running down her face and her mouth wide open.

"Good thinking, bruh," I said, giving Dak dap. Amoy turned into a crazy woman trying to beat Dak for scaring her shitless. She was crying, cussing and throwing punches at him. All he did was laugh and shield his body from her punches until she caught him with one to his lip. The blood dripping from his lip made him calm Amoy's ass down quickly. He held her in a bear hug as she squirmed to get away from him.

"I'm sorry. Now, calm da fuck down. Yo brother wasn't ready to do that shit, so I just did what I could," he said softly to her. She finally stopped fighting him and started crying like a newborn baby.

"I thought you were dying," she said through her sobs. He held her while kissing all over her face until she stopped crying. Amoy was still dramatic as hell.

"Nigga, you made me lose two hundred dollars," Cache said staring at me.

"Man, I thought you was dying for real until you opened your eyes. I almost fell out laughing at that shit," Noble said laughing. Everyone started laughing except Amoy and me. I could feel her eyes burning a hole through me.

"It ain't funny. You just ruined what was supposed to be the happiest day of that girl's life. You owe her an apology and explanation," she said angrily to me. "I may've not wanted you to marry her but that was just wrong, Jarvis."

"I know. I'll sit down and talk with her," I said calmly. Everything she said was the truth. I shouldn't have let it get this far.

There were only two people in this world that I never wanted to look at me with disappointment. One of them was staring me dead in the eyes right now.

Memories of the night that I took Aunt Belle from her flashed through my mind. When I found out Aunt Belle was responsible for our parents' deaths, she had to die. I never considered how her death would affect me and Amoy's relationship. Amoy had forgiven me, but I still felt a disconnect between us. My feelings stayed bottled up inside until I was with Nova. She would sit and listen to me talk for hours about how losing my parents and killing Aunt Belle fucked me up. Still, Nova walked away from me when I needed her the most. I felt my chest getting tight and needed air. Everyone in the limo was quiet because they could feel the tension between Amoy and me.

"You need to fix this. And I'm not only talking about Valentine. Whatever unresolved issues and feelings you have with Nova, you need to handle them. Ever since she left, you went from living life with a death wish to a completely different person. I mean don't get me wrong, I love the person you've become, but you need to get your personal life together."

I couldn't argue with her because everything she said was the truth.

"You want me to fix the fucked-up way Nova left?" I asked staring at her.

"She didn't leave you in anyway. You never gave her a reason to stay," she said. "And yes, Jarvis, do whatever you have to do."

I pushed the intercom for the chauffer and told him to pull over.

"Where you going?" Amoy asked.

I ignored her and stepped out of the limo. I called Bahka. He was my driver and bodyguard when necessary. I didn't trust many, but I trusted him with my life.

The Next Morning

My head was pounding when I woke up the next morning. The last thing I remembered last night was coming to my condo and emptying a bottle of cognac down my throat. I couldn't remember how I ended up with

Valentine lying beside me naked. I eased out of the bed without waking her. While in the shower, I tried remembering what happened last night. It finally dawned on me, but I still didn't remember Valentine coming over. My mind was so far gone, I didn't hear Valentine come in the bathroom. She opened the shower door and stepped in dropping to her knees. My dick was limp until she started massaging it with her tongue. It became semi-hard until she took it inside her mouth. My dick was brick hard by the time I started ramming it against her throat. I gripped a handful of her hair and started fucking her mouth. She was gagging, slurping and sucking every inch until I unloaded inside her mouth. We showered together and she stepped out of the shower.

"I'll be waiting for you downstairs to discuss the embarrassing way you left me at our wedding," she said, wrapping a towel around her. I had planned on giving her a few days to calm down, but I guess she wasn't as mad as I thought.

After getting out of the shower, I slipped on a pair of boxers and sweats. The shower woke me up, but my head was still pounding from the hangover, so I took three Tylenol pills before making my way downstairs. Valentine was seated at the kitchen table sipping coffee and scrolling through her phone. She rolled her eyes at me as I walked past her to make myself a cup of coffee. I could feel her eyes on me as I poured the coffee.

"Who is Nova?" she asked. Her question caused me to drop the entire pot of coffee on the counter. "Well, at least I know she's someone relevant to you."

I forgot the coffee and walked over and sat across from her.

"Why do you ask about her?" I asked.

"Because you fucked me into an oblivion last night while calling her name. I should've been beyond furious but the way you were fucking me I would've been a fool to stop the orgasms you were giving me," she said with a smile.

"I don't remember calling you to come over," I said.

"I know. I was furious, hurt and embarrassed so I came over to cuss you out. You had other things on your mind," she said smiling, referring to the sex we had. "For a minute, I thought you regretted jilting me but then you started saying her name over and over."

Nona Day   Over You

"I'll accommodate you for emotional distress, but I can't marry you," I said bluntly. She didn't need to know anything about Nova, so I wanted to change the topic.

"Two million and I'll make you sound like an angel to the blogs," she said. "A man of your caliber doesn't need any bad publicity. It's hard enough getting the elite privilege to accept you as is," she said with quotation gestures around elite privilege.

She was right. It took me a while to be taking serious by the most prominent people in Atlanta. It wasn't only the whites that looked at me sideways. I caught hell from my own people as well. Some of them were harder on me than my white colleagues.

I chuckled. "I paid for everything in the wedding. You keep the engagement ring and one million."

She smiled. "We could've made a great team. I saw us making our way to the White House."

It was a possibility with her ambition and my power in Atlanta and its surrounding states, but I had no interest in getting into politics. If people started digging too deep into my background, I'd end up behind bars. But I was happy to have politicians in my pockets for favors. I still ran the strongest drug organization in the south, but I also owned several malls, casinos, hotels and other businesses under my company, Galaxy Enterprise.

"I'll be expecting that money in my account by the end of the day," she said, standing up. She walked over, leaned down and kissed me on the lips. "Call me whenever you start to miss Nova again."

I chuckled and shook my head. Here I was feeling like shit for hurting her, but the only love she had for me was the places we could go as a couple. Her ambition was sexy but wasn't enough for me to promise to spend the rest of my life with her.

After Valentine left, I went into my man cave. I didn't know what it was lately, but a lot had been weighing on my mind about my life. I had enough money to do any and everything I wanted yet I still felt empty. I had people in my life that loved me, but I still felt like I wasn't worthy of their love.

I needed to blow off my steam, so I headed to one of the gyms I had opened. I had taken a couple of weeks off for the honeymoon; since that was canceled I decided to dive back into work. I was going to give the tickets to

Valentine, so she could enjoy the vacation with whoever she chose.

Nova started this shit and some kind of way she was going to fix what she fucked up inside of me.

SOUL Publications

Nova

$\mathcal{I}$ sat on the balcony of my small apartment doing my afternoon yoga. The October's air was chilly in Dothan, Alabama. Since leaving Atlanta two years ago, Dothan had been my home. I lasted only three months at the job that caused me to move here. The corporate world just wasn't for me. It was stressful, time consuming and overwhelming. One thing kept me from moving back to Atlanta after I quit. Jarvis left an ache in my heart that I still felt two years later. We had built a special kind of friendship that I wanted to grow into so much more.

The night Amoy told him I was leaving I honestly hadn't decided if I was going to take the job. My plans were to talk with Jarvis about our relationship. I thought what we had was special. Even if he didn't want a romantic relationship with me, our friendship should've been strong enough that he wanted me to stay. He dismissed me like I was one of his countless one-night-stands. Jarvis and I spent many days and nights at his condo with me just listening to him share his deepest feelings about his parents and Aunt Belle's deaths. He never told me why he chose me to share such intimate thoughts with, but I didn't need to know the reason why. I enjoyed every minute I got to spend with him.

Jarvis wasn't the type of guy that I would normally fall for. Being somewhat eccentric, spiritual and free-spirited I normally was attracted to nerds, gentlemen and guys that matched my vibes. Jar was none of those things. He was rude, annoying, angry and crazy as a bat. He was intimidating to a dorky, country girl like me but so intriguing. There was an energy inside of him that pulled me in and wouldn't release me. Every time I was in his presence, I could feel a magnetic pull forcing me to be near him. I thought moving to Dothan would help me get over the crush I had on him, but I was still like a lovesick puppy. We never had a sexual relationship. Well, there was that one time after the gala event. After that night, he slowly started to pull away from me, and I didn't know why. Remembering that night between us made me smile, but I was sad at the same time.

Nona Day   Over You

We had such a great time at the gala that night, I just knew the night was going to end perfectly. When one of his female friends called while we rode in the back of the limo, he agreed to come to her place for a quickie. It was very late, so he took me back to his place instead of my parents' house. It would've been the first time he saw my little she shed that I lived in. He had never been to my parents' house because I was spending most of my time at his place.

A couple of hours later, Jar was banging on the spare bedroom door that I occupied when I slept over. After Aunt Belle's death, I was on edge thinking something more horrible had happened. A totally intoxicated Jarvis stood on the other side of the door barely able to stand with his head hanging low. He finally looked up at me and something in his eyes made my womanhood thud.

"Fuck Nova," he said in a low, raspy voice. When he licked his lips, I realized what caused the salacious look in his eyes. I was standing at the door completely naked. The only time I slept in clothes was during my monthly cycle. His banging on the door made me forget to put on some clothes.

I tried to quickly walk away and grab something to cover myself, but he grabbed my arm. Never asking my permission, he staggered inside and covered my mouth with his, sliding his tongue inside my slightly open mouth. I tasted a blend of cognac, weed, mints and sweet saliva on his tongue. His strong masculine hands started massaging my B-cup breasts. My flower started to fill with wetness and my nipples started to harden. Soft moans escaped me as I enjoyed our first kiss. My body was heating up with every second that passed. I wrapped my arms around his neck. His masculine hands started exploring the contour of my body while his tongue tasted the flavor of my neck. He pinned me against the bedroom wall securing my arms over my head. The erotic, sensual way his tongue licked, sucked and nibbled on my breasts caused my nectar to spill down between my inner thighs. I could hear low grunts coming from him as he pressed his body against mine. The hard bulge in his black trousers poked into my belly.

"Aaaahh," I moaned when he slipped his hand between my wet thighs. Letting my arms go, he started nibbling on my earlobe. A finger slipped between my two petals causing my knees to buckle. He quickly wrapped a hand around my waist to hold me up. I was like putty in his hands.

"*I smell your pussy juice. I wanna fuck you so damn bad, Nova,*" he groaned as he started kissing his way down my body. *This was what I'd wanted since the day I met him, but for some reason this didn't feel right. I remembered he had left me here to go have sex with another woman. He came back to me a drunken mess and I needed to know why. It took all the moral dignity I had to stop him from giving me what my body had craved from him for so long.*

"*Jarvis no,*" I said trying to push his head away. *He looked up at me with so much sadness and desperation in his eyes.*

"*Come on, Nova. I need this shit right now,*" he pleaded with me. *Jarvis wanted sex with me to take away the torture inside of him. Us having sex would only satisfy him for the moment and rip my soul apart, because I knew it was only sex he wanted from me. Seeing the most intimidating man I had ever met look so vulnerable caused tears to fill my eyes. I stared down at him with sympathetic eyes.*

"*I can't, Jarvis,*" I said remorsefully. *Jar stood up and stared at me with rage in his eyes. A loud yelp came from me when he angrily rammed his fist into the wall causing a hole. He walked out of the bedroom leaving me standing there shook by seeing that side of him. I'd heard many stories about Jarvis' temper, but he was always calm with me.*

I slipped on a pair of pajama shorts and a tank top before making my way downstairs. I found Jarvis in the kitchen guzzling down a bottle of cognac. When he sat the bottle on the kitchen isle, I took it and put it in the cabinet. He walked away from me without saying a word and sat in the dark living room. I prepared a cup of my specialty blended herbal tea for him and joined him on the sofa.

"You wanna talk about it?" I asked, giving him the cup of tea.

"Nah, but you can put some of that liquid weed in here," he said.

I laughed. "Not tonight. I'm going to give you a natural high."

"Shit, I thought you was too, but you stopped me," he said, rolling his eyes at me.

"Just sit here and drink the tea until I get back," I said, standing up.

Nona Day   Over You

I went to my bedroom and prepared a place by the window for meditation. I was at his place so much, I had to make sure I kept necessities here also. Two pillows lay on the floor surrounded by different crystals. I lit several candles before turning the lights off.

Jarvis was texting on a small flip phone when I walked back into the living room. I took the phone from his hand and placed it on the table. His eyes were glued to my body.

"So we fucking?" he asked looking up at me.

"No. Now, come with me," I said taking his hand. He followed me to my bedroom and immediately flipped out, turning the bedroom light on.

"Nova, I ain't trying to judge what kind of God you serve. I ain't the most religious type of nigga myself, but I don't do this witchcraft shit," he said looking around.

"I'm not a witch. This is just meditation, but I understand if this is something you don't want to try," I said.

"I mean I'll try it as long as we ain't cutting chicken necks and drinking blood," he said seriously. I laughed and turned the light back off.

"You need to be as comfortable as possible. Remove your shoes and pants," I told him.

"Nah can't do that. My dick hard enough to break through a steel wall," he said seriously.

I laughed and said, "I've seen hard ones before. It won't scare me. Plus, it's only right that I see you now."

He shrugged his shoulders and stripped down to his boxers. My eyes grew wide as I stared at the enormous swollen manhood under his boxers. I couldn't take my eyes off of it. Words were coming from his mouth, but my only focus was on the jewels I'd dreamt about so many nights. Placing his hand under my chin, he lifted my face to get my attention.

"It's probably best we don't fuck. I heard skinny girls can't take big dicks," he said with a devilish grin. I doubt if any woman could take what he was offering. I laughed and gently pushed him in his broad, muscular chest.

"Shut up," I said jokingly. My eyes traveled down to his feet. "You have pretty feet."

"My dick prettier. You wanna see it?" he asked, grabbing his crotch. He was shocked when I nodded my head, but wasted no time dropping his boxers and stepping

out of them. I watched as he held the most beautiful,
chocolate penis that I'd ever seen. I had been face to face
with only two others, but I'd seen plenty on porn sites.
Jarvis' manhood with massive with length and width. The
thickness of it made my flower clench at the thought of it
entering me. The mushroom shaped head was perfect and a
shade lighter than the shaft. The thick veins running
through the shaft looked like roots from a big oak tree.

"You ready?" he asked staring at me, pulling me out
of my trance. He smiled at me and pulled his T-shirt over
his head. I prayed to my ancestors to help me stay focused,
because this man's body was a sinful, beautiful distraction.
The ripped abs, deep V, broad chest, and muscular,
tattooed arms resembled a sculpted Egyptian God.

"Sit on the pillow in the most comfortable position," I
said, sitting down with my legs crossed.

"Promise not to hurt me," he said, winking at me. I
smiled and shook my head. He sat across from me in the
same manner.

"Close your eyes and concentrate on relaxing every
part of your body. Starting from the top of your head to the
soles of your feet. Think of places, people or memories that

bring peace into your mind," I instructed while doing the same for myself.

Memories of my childhood flashed through my mind. Spending quality time working with my father on the farm, cooking in the kitchen with my mother, and skinny dipping in the small lake on my parents' farm took me to a place of complete peace. We meditated for approximately ten minutes. When I opened my eyes, Jar was staring at me. I started to get angry that he didn't at least try to meditate with me, but the tranquility in his eyes revealed a harmonious glare I'd never seen in him before.

"You meditated with your eyes opened?" I asked.

"It was necessary," he said still glaring at me. Everyone meditated differently, so who was I to judge.

"How do you feel?" I asked.

"Light," he replied looking down. "I fucking came on myself."

I looked to see his thick, milky cum on his brawny thigh. My salacious appetite for him had me wondering if his cum was as sweet as his saliva. I looked up and smiled at him.

Nona Day   Over You

"I gotta get da fuck outta here," he said quickly standing up. He didn't bother to gather his clothes, slamming the door behind him.

That was the night he slowly started to drift away from me. Today, he was heavy on my mind because I was returning back home to surprise my parents for their anniversary. I hadn't taken a trip home in over a year, but always kept in touch with Amoy and Cache. They agreed to never discuss Jarvis with me, because they knew how much I cared about him. It crushed my heart when I heard that he was getting married on the radio. Jarvis was a millionaire powerhouse in Atlanta and was becoming well-known everywhere. I'd never been the jealous type or had low self-esteem, but I often wondered what she had to offer him that I didn't. What made him love and want to commit to her, but not me? That was one of the things that scared me. Jarvis gave me self-doubt within myself. It took moving away to find the Goddess within myself again.

Later That Evening

Nona Day   Over You

I had planned to be at my parents' house by now, but my unorganized life wouldn't let that happen. Working as a virtual assistant caused me to have to complete a few jobs before I left. It was almost nine o'clock and I was speeding through the back roads in my 2017 Smart Fortwo. It was a gift from my parents when I moved to Alabama. Ma was so happy about me choosing to give the corporate world another try.

I loved traveling back roads. It gave me time to think and clear my mind. My intentions were to enjoy the beautiful scenery but traveling at night ruined that. All I could see was the road ahead of me. My heart dropped to the pit of my stomach when an enormous deer leaped out in front of my car. I quickly swerved my steering wheel but wasn't able to avoid it. The deer swiped the side of my car and landed on my hood.

Frantically, I jerked the steering wheel trying to throw the deer off of the hood. I was successful, but sent my car spending out of control. The next thing I remember was seeing car lights and a white man walking toward me. I didn't know if I should've been scared for my life or thankful someone had come to save me. I was able to see my car turned over in the ditch, but I was lying on side of the road feeling like a semi had run into me. The white man scooped me from the ground and put me in the backseat of his car. He never said a word to me before I felt his car moving. Tears filled my eyes; I was in fear of what was going to happen to me. The pounding in my head was excruciating and caused me to become dizzy. It wasn't long before I blacked out.

Jarvis

"*E*xcuse me for a minute," I said to one of my business partners. "I need to take this call."

After hitting the gym, I went out for drinks to discuss an upcoming project with him. I couldn't ignore the call because it was from my private investigator. I stepped out of the restaurant to answer his call.

"Yea," I answered. He had called me earlier to inform me that Nova was on the road headed in this direction.

"She was in a car accident," he informed me. A rush of heat spread through my body. My heart started to pound, and I could feel myself starting to sweat.

"What hospital they take her to?" I asked. I had so many questions, but my only concern right now was making sure she was okay and got the best care possible.

"She was about forty-five miles out of Atlanta on a deserted road. She doesn't seem to have any serious injuries, but she has blacked out in the backseat of my car. What do you want me to do?"

Nona Day   Over You

"Break every gah-damn speed limit and run every light until you get to my house. I'll text you the address," I said ending the call. I immediately sent him to my house where I hardly ever stayed. I spent most of my time at my condominium. Completely forgetting about the meeting I was having, I hopped in my car and headed to my house. I called my on-call personal doctor to meet me there.

When I arrived at the house, I paced the floor anxiously. Worry mixed with my anxiety caused my mind to be in overdrive. I hadn't laid eyes on Nova in two years. I'd seen numerous pictures but to be in her presence had me shook. When I heard the doorbell ring, my entire body froze. It felt as if I could feel the pounding of my heart in my gut. I forced my feet to move and went to open the door. A huge sigh of relief came over me when I saw it was Doc. Stepping to the side, I allowed him to walk in.

"Where is she?" he asked. Without giving him an answer, I called Trevor.

"Pulling in through the gates," he said. I ended the call without replying because nerves had taken over every inch of my body.

"Do you need a sedative?" Doc asked staring at me. I almost told him I did until I heard a car horn blowing. Doc followed behind me as we made our way out the house. Trevor was opening the back door when we approached the car.

"She's still knocked out," he said, bending down to pick her up.

"Don't touch her!" I barked, pushing him out the way. I took a deep breath and bent down to look at her. Blood was on the side of her face; her clothes were dirty, and bruises and scratches were on her arms. Yet, she looked like a priceless African painting lying in her colorful pants and checkered blouse. I almost chuckled when I looked at the hideous, metallic purple, thick heeled shoes on her feet. Nova had the weirdest style ever.

"We need to get her inside to examine her," Doc said standing beside me. Carefully and gently, I scooped her out of the backseat of the car and carried her inside. She was still unconscious, and I started to worry.

"Why da fuck she not waking up?" I asked Doc. The moment I asked the question with her in my arms, her eyes slowly started to open. She quickly blinked her eyes a few more times before staring at me.

"Jarvis?" As soon as she said my name, she blacked out again.

The way she said my name was filled with curiosity, endearment and shock but all I heard was the most soothing, seductive melody.

"Jarvis, you have to lay her down so I can examine her," Doc reminded me.

I took her to the third floor of my house. She was knocked out the entire time. After lying her down, I stepped out the room to let Doc examine her. Trevor was standing in the hall.

"What happened?" I asked.

"I was trailing her but made sure not to get too close. She took all the back roads trying to get here. I'm not sure how she flipped the car," he said, shaking his head. "The car was flipped on its side in the ditch while she was lying on side of the road. She didn't lose consciousness until I pulled off with her in the backseat of my car."

"I'm just glad you were there. You can go. I'll make sure you're compensated for your time," I said, leaning against the wall.

"I called a tow truck for the car. I'll text you the address as to where she can locate it," he informed me.

"Was she driving that small ass toy car?" I asked. He chuckled and nodded his head. "Tell whoever to use it for parts or return it back to the toy store. She shouldn't have been driving a Toys R Us car on those damn dark roads."

"A'ight. Just let me know if you need me," he said, leaving me in my thoughts. I needed a drink to calm my nerves, but I was glued to my bedroom door. The last thing I wanted to do was upset her when she saw me. I was sure a million questions would be running through her mind.

It took Doc about thirty minutes before he walked out of the room.

"How is she?" I asked.

"Bruised up. No concussion, so no need to keep her woke. I gave her something for the pain, so she'll be knocked out for the night. Bring her in first thing in the morning for X-rays. I doubt if there is any, but I want to check her for internal bleeding. If she wakes up coughing blood take her to the ER," he informed me.

"Does she know I'm here. Does she know where she's at?" I asked.

"No to both questions. I noticed how anxious she got when she mentioned she thought she saw you, so I told her it was from the hit on her head," he replied. "That headache is going to be massive in the morning. I left some more pain pills on the nightstand."

"Thanks. I'll take care of the bill in the morning," I said.

"Never worry about that with you," he said smiling at me. We shook hands before he left. She was sound asleep under the covers when I walked in the room. After dimming the lights, I walked over and stood over her. I'd always wondered what it would feel like to have her in my bed, but never imagined it would be like this.

After taking in as much of her as my eyes would allow, I made my way to the bedroom beside my master bedroom. With her on my mind, I couldn't sleep. My mind started to remember how she left. All the worry I had for her started to anger me. She left me broken, so I shouldn't be concerned about her. The only thing I wanted to do was get her out of my system. She wasn't leaving this house until I was over her.

Nona Day   Over You

The Next Morning

This shit gotta stop! I screamed the words in my head getting out of my bed. Here I was over thirty years old and having wet damn dreams about her. There wasn't a woman in the city of Atlanta that wouldn't mind fucking me, but my whipped ass was drooling over pussy I never had. After taking a quick shower, I didn't give myself enough time to analyze my next move as I made my way to the master bedroom. *This shit ends today.*

I turned the doorknob thinking I was going to walk into the room and wake her ass up, but I was shocked to find the door locked. Before I could bang on the door, it came flying open. She stood there in one of my black T-shirts with her angelic smile. Her wild hair was dripping wet. Without a drop of make up on her face she was the most beautiful creation I had ever laid eyes on.

"Jarvis." She said my name with the same melody from last night. I was like a young schoolboy: tongue tied, nervous and awe struck by the prettiest girl in school.

She threw her arms around me and I felt like my body was floating in midair. My mind told me to push her away, but my heart and dick were tag teaming my thoughts. Ignoring the screaming to deny her warm, loving greeting I wrapped my arms around her small waist. While holding her in my arms, I tried to think of what in my life had ever felt better, but nothing could compare. My thoughts weren't sexual. They weren't even about her. All I felt was a peaceful feeling I hadn't felt after my parents died.

"Thank you for saving me," she whispered with her lips pressed against my neck. Nova wasn't short; standing at least five foot eight inches. My six foot three inches still had an advantage. I felt her start to release me. Not wanting this moment to end, my arms held her tighter. Several minutes later, I let her go. With the same smile, she stepped back staring at me. She carefully held her side and I could see a look of anguish over her face. I had been holding her as tight as I could with her bruised, sore body.

"Seeing you made me forget about how much pain I was in. I didn't know where I was this morning, and barely could remember what happened to me. After a while, everything started to come back to me," she rambled. "I thought maybe I was dreaming about seeing you last night until I rummaged the dresser for a T-shirt. The scent of the clothes told me I wasn't dreaming last night. Hope you don't mind."

I couldn't reply because I was stuck in a trance by her. The fact that she was in my bedroom, with my T-shirt and boxers on was surreal. So many nights I'd dreamed about moments like this.

"This bedroom is enormous. My apartment and the ones on each side of me can fit in here," she said looking around the ceiling. Her eyes met mine again and we just stood there absorbing each other until an awkward expression fell over her face.

"I know you have a lot to do, so I'll get out of your way," she said nervously. "Was my phone retrieved from the accident?"

"No and that little toy ass car is totaled. You need to eat something before you take the painkillers," I said walking over to the dresser. I placed the bottle of pills in her hand. "The breakfast room is on the bottom floor," I finally spoke. Not giving her a chance to reply, I walked out of the room.

I had a full staff of housekeepers, a chef and gardener to attend to the house where I never stayed. This would've been me and Valentine's home had I married her. When I walked in the kitchen, my chef, Antoine was still preparing breakfast. Antoine was a white cook at one of my favorite restaurants. He got into a huge fight with the owner one night and was fired, so I hired him to be my personal chef.

"It's been three weeks since you've ate here," he said looking over his shoulder. Normally, Antoine would meal prep for me and send the food over to my condo.

"I'll be here for a few days, so prepare to earn your money. There's a guest staying so accommodate her needs and wants," I informed him. He simply nodded his head.

About thirty minutes later, I was sitting in the breakfast room getting ready to eat when Nova walked in. She had spent time taming her hair by putting it into four big, long plaits.

"Sorry it took so long," she said, sitting at the big circular table. "I got lost."

"Eat," I said.

"Wow," she said staring at the variety of food on the table. She bowed her head and prayed over the food. Neither of us spoke a word as we ate. Nova stuffed herself with fresh fruit, omelets, and crepes. She didn't touch the sausage and bacon because she didn't eat pork, so I made a mental note to inform Antoine.

"Now take your medicine," I instructed her. I could tell she was in pain.

"I would prefer some herbal medicine," she said with a coy smile. I couldn't help but chuckled. Nova loved smoking out as much as me. We'd shared many smoke sessions together. During those times, she listened to me without judgment.

"I have some in my man cave," I told her.

"Thank you again, Jarvis. I was so scared," she said looking across the table at me. I simply nodded my head. "You have a breathtaking home. Well, the little of it I've glimpsed at."

"I'll make sure you get a tour later," I answered

"Can I ask you a question?" she asked shyly. I nodded my head.

"How did I end up here?" she asked.

I didn't care that what I was about to say was going to freak her out. I'd had to deal with her leaving for two years. Now, she was going to deal with me until I said it was over.

Nova

"For two damn years I've been stuck under some spell since you left. I needed to know how you were doing and if you were safe, so I hired a PI to keep tabs on you. He's been keeping me updated for the past year and was trailing you last night. Since your injuries weren't serious, I ordered him to bring you here. After breakfast, we'll be going to see my doctor for a follow up," he said nonchalantly.

My mouth slowly fell open as I tried to wrap my brain around what he was saying to me. So many questions were running through my head. I should've been running out of his house after hearing what he had just said, but I wasn't scared of him. If he wanted to hurt me, he would've done it already. Jarvis was protective of his friends and family. Regardless of how we left each other, I knew he still considered me a friend.

"Jarvis, I'm not understanding what's going on. Why am I here?" I asked still confused.

"You're here because I want you here," he said, standing up. "I have a personal assistant that'll be here with some clothes for you. Make a list of hygiene, hair care, and beauty supplies you need."

He walked out of the breakfast room leaving me sitting there in disbelief of what was going on. I still didn't understand what he wanted from me. There was no way he was going to keep me trapped in this exquisite, unbelievably beautiful home against my will with no explanation. If he needed my help with something, I'd be more than willing to assist him. But not like this. I drug my battered and sore body through the house calling his name. The house was so enormous my echoes could be heard repeatedly. I finally found him in the walk-in closet of what I assumed was the master bedroom.

"I still don't understand. Why do you want me here, Jarvis?" I asked, walking inside the closet that was the size of my one-bedroom apartment if not bigger. I took a quick moment to scan all the overly expensive clothes and shoes. Something clicked in my head. There were no casual street clothes that I was used to seeing Jarvis wearing. I finally noticed how Jarvis' entire demeanor had changed. He was somewhat poised, polished, and cavalier. This wasn't the Jarvis that I remembered.

He walked up to me and stared down at me.

"Take that voodoo ass spell off of me and you can leave," he said seriously, making my eyes stretch in disbelief. He didn't wait for my reply as he walked out of the closet.

"What?" I asked puzzled, following behind him. I glanced at the crème colored cashmere sweater, black trousers and loafers on the off-white bench chair at the end of the extra-large King size bed I slept in last night.

"You heard what da fuck I said, Nova! Take that shit off of me and you can go home!"

I couldn't believe how serious he was. He actually thought I put a spell on him. I'd never practiced witchcraft a day in my life. I burst out laughing because I thought this moment was pure comical. A simple laugh made my head start throbbing and my body ache more. He rushed up to me, yoking me around my slender, long neck with one hand.

"You think this shit is funny?" He asked through gritted teeth.

Nona Day   Over You

His body oozed with masculine, woodsy cologne. The look in his eyes bought back so many memories of why I had fallen so hard for him. Jarvis was everything I wasn't. He was reckless, mean, demanding, rude and domineering. My flower jumped at the feel of the bulge in his pajama pants pressed against my stomach. I should've been fearing my life at this moment, but all I wanted was to feel his lips against mine. Two years later, he still had the same effect on me. My flower started to water itself at thoughts of him being inside me. My thoughts were downright sinful for this man. He belonged to another woman, but that didn't matter to me at the moment. I knew I was wrong, but I couldn't stop myself.

I slowly reached up and held his wrist with my eyes glaring up into his. His grip slowly eased from around my neck until he let me go. My mind knew everything I wanted from him was wrong, but my body had to have him. I started placing soft kisses into the palm of his hand hoping he didn't reject me. The anger in his eyes gradually softened, turning into lust. His free hand slid up his long T-shirt that I wore. Shivers traveled through my body as his fingers tickled my flesh. Placing my other hand against the side of his face, I ran my thumb across his soft, full lips.

His face moved closer to me until his lips gently touched my lips.

When he slipped his thick, warm tongue inside my mouth, electrifying sensations shot through me and detonated in my core. A simple erotic gesture with his mouth caused my nectar to overflow. Sucking my tongue into his wet mouth, both his hands found their way under the T-shirt. Massaging my breasts and pinching my hard nipples turned my soft moans into cries of pleasure. I tugged at the knot I had tied in his oversized boxers I had on, making them fall to the floor. Every moral fiber in my body abandoned me in this moment. His lips left my mouth and his tongue ravished my neck. Breaking away from my neck only to pull the T-shirt over my head, he attacked my breasts like a starved man. My juices seeped from my core and slid down my inner thighs as he licked, sucked and nibbled on my breasts.

His strong arms lifted me up, and I wrapped my legs around his waist. I was so hyped with sex driven adrenaline; I felt no pain from my bruised body. Never taking his mouth from my breasts, he walked me over to the bed and laid me down. I laid spread eagle across the bed ready to feel what I'd wanted for two years. My injured body was ready to endure the pain to feel his pleasure. My morals and regret would reappear after this was over. I'd deal with the repercussions then. I watched as he removed his tank top and pulled down his pajama pants.

I could feel my center beckoning for him. The perfect visual of his massive, beautiful rod was still engraved in my mind, but looking at it in this moment was scary. I hadn't been intimate with a man in over three years. This was going to be a challenge, but I wasn't backing down. He laid on top of me using his elbows to keep his torso over my body. He glared down at me as if he was waiting for me to stop this from happening. There was no doubt in my eyes. Leaning down he ran his tongue across my lips. My legs reacted by lifting and wrapping around his waist. Placing his weapon at my opening, my body stiffened with anticipation. He kissed his way to my left earlobe and started nibbling.

"Relax. Open up for me, Nova," he whispered in my ear. His voice was full of ecstasy and agony.

My body started to relax as he licked and sucked all over my neck. The feeling of his mushroom head tearing through my opening was painfully blissful. All the aches in my body were no comparison. He lifted his head and stared down at me. Taking my legs from around his waist, he slowly and gently spread them apart. The rest of his manhood struggled to get inside me as my flower poured nectar like a running faucet. The pain of him entering me was no matched for the overwhelming feeling in my heart. I had never felt anything so exhilarating and gratifying. Tears started to fill my eyes as he slid deeper in my tunnel. Our eyes locked on each other, and time stopped for only a brief moment. His rod was pulsating against my walls. Jar's eyes looked discombobulated. I reached up and caressed the side of his face because he looked so confused and helpless.

"Nova," he groaned my name painfully before his body started to convulse. I could feel his semen pumping through his shaft as he came inside of me.

"Jar, I know…. OH SHIT!" Amoy said, barging inside the bedroom.

"Get da fuck out!" Jarvis barked, collapsing on top of me as if he was trying to cover my body. I wanted to scream out in pain. All the aches came back ten times fold with all of his weight on me.

"My bad. I'll be waiting downstairs in the den. Hi Nova, glad you're back," Amoy said, closing the door behind her. I couldn't help but giggle.

Jarvis didn't say a word to me when he stood up. He never even looked at me before going to the bathroom to clean himself up. After a few minutes in the bathroom, he came out and put his jammies and tank top back on. He walked out of the room. I noticed my clothes had been washed as they lie folded on the chair in the corner of the room. As I tried getting out of bed, I felt the soreness between my legs and body. It was only a couple of minutes of heaven, but it felt like he had pulverized my insides for hours. Tingling sensations traveled through me making me bite my bottom lip because those couple of minutes sent me to the stars. I didn't have time to fully reflect on our first and possibly last time together, because I wanted to see Amoy.

About thirty minutes later, I joined Nova and Jarvis in the den. I couldn't get over how elegantly designed the house was. Jarvis was a simple guy. At least the Jarvis I remembered.

"Nova!" Amoy ran over toward me.

"Don't hug her too damn tight!" Jarvis barked at her. "She's got a lot of aches."

"Didn't stop you," Amoy said, looking over her shoulder at me. He looked the other way. I wanted to laugh but held it. She walked over and wrapped her arms around me for a warm, comforting hug. I returned the hug because I was so elated to see her. Jarvis sat on the sofa scanning through his phone.

"I'm so happy to see you," I told her. "How did you know it was me?

"Me too. And only you would wear metallic stack shoes," she said finally breaking our embrace and looking over her shoulder at Jarvis. He looked up at her with a scowl on his face. "I can't believe this nutcase has been stalking you. But I'm glad he was. He told me about the accident."

"Yea, I hope the deer survived as well," I said.

Amoy laughed. "I'm sure that lil car of yours only bumped it." I had sent her pictures of my car when my parents bought it. She thought it was the cutest little toy.

"Amoy, didn't you say you had an appointment or something?" Jarvis asked, standing up.

"Nigga, don't be trying to rush me off," she said, waving him off.

"You leaving already?" I asked.

"I'm leaving but I'm going to call you tomorrow, so we can meet up with Cache for drinks," she assured me.

"No you won't. I got shit I need to handle with Nova without you and Cache's interference. So say your goodbyes, because this will be the last time you see her for a while," Jarvis said seriously.

"What?" Amoy asked confused.

"Jarvis thinks I got some kind of spell on him, so he's holding me hostage until I remove it," I said with a smile. I still thought it was comical.

He walked up to me. "You still think that shit funny?"

If whatever he had planned for me involved what happened about an hour ago, I never wanted to be released. I chose to keep that thought to myself.

"Jar, you fuckin' insane. You can't keep her locked in here," Amoy spat angrily.

"Ain't you the one that told me to resolve shit between us?" He asked looking at Amoy. "That's what I'm doing."

"Fool, not like this," she said angrily.

"Go home, Amoy," Jarvis said, walking past us. We watched him walk out the den and disappear.

"Go get your things. I'm sorry about this," Amoy said sympathetically to me.

"It's okay, Amoy. Jarvis needs me for something. Not sure what that is, but I care enough about him to stay and help," I answered.

She smiled. "You still in love with him."

I never stopped loving him and now I doubt if I ever will.

Jarvis came back with a short, young, white girl. She carried an iPad and was neatly dressed in a two-piece, short skirt set with her hair pinned back in a ponytail.

"This Sandy. Let her know what all you need. She's going to help you shop for some clothes and shoes as well," Jarvis informed me.

"I can't believe you're actually serious, Jarvis," Amoy said looking at him in disbelief.

"Some things I don't buy online, Jarvis. I need to visit the store to purchase them. Like my crystals, candles and incense."

"Nah, ain't no voodoo shit being done here," he said staring at me.

"That is her belief. You can't possibly be that cruel or crazy," Amoy said, stepping in his face. He stared at me to see how sad the thought of not being able to practice my daily rituals made me.

"Fine! I'll take you later to whatever store you need to go to," he said, walking away. Amoy followed behind him.

I knew it was bizarre that I was willing to go along with whatever Jarvis was doing, but maybe he wasn't the only one who needed this. I'd been pining over him for the past two years. Every guy that attempted to make a connection with me left before I even knew what happened. Maybe we needed to get each other out of our systems so we could move on. The problem with that for me was this thing I had for Jarvis was more than sex. Jarvis needed healing and for some reason he thought he could get that from me. I was willing to risk walking away with a shattered heart to help him and fulfill the need I had for him.

Nona Day   Over You

Sandy and I sat in the living room going through websites full of clothes that were outrageously overpriced and totally not my style. Nothing on the sites caught my eye.

A few minutes later, Amoy walked back into the living room.

"When you've had enough of this foolishness, give me a call," she said bluntly. I stood up and gave her a hug before saying goodbye.

Jarvis walked back into the den.

"Jarvis, I don't like any of those clothes. I shop at thrift stores and consignment shops," I informed him.

"While you're here, I advise you to pick out some clothes with Sandy or walk around the house naked every day," he replied before walking away.

I looked back at Sandy. "Thank you, but I won't be needing your assistance."

Jarvis was getting dressed when I walked into the bedroom. Even though the comforter on the bed was black I could still see my wetness that had seeped in. I wanted to mention what had happened between us, but I didn't want to make a big deal about it. I was sure it was just sex for Jarvis.

"Are there any house rules?" I asked.

"Give Antoine a list of your likes and dislikes. The housekeeping staff works from seven AM to three PM Monday through Thursday. Only the top housekeeper, Rochelle, lives here. She stays in the west wing. She's the only one that cleans the third floor between the hours of ten and twelve, no one and I mean no one is allowed on the third floor but her, me and you. Antoine will be coming and going for meals. The gardener comes once a week," he informed me. "If you need to go anywhere, Bahka will take you. No visiting my sister or Cache. As for as your parents know, you're on a spiritual retreat for a while. Take time to explore your dwelling unit for the time being."

I didn't know who Bahka was, but I was sure I'd find out. At least my parents weren't worried about me.

"You talked to my parents? You have my phone?" I asked. That was the only way he could've pretended to be me by texting them.

"Yes, cheap shit cracked," he answered truthfully. "Jesus, Nova, who still owns a Motorola?"

Nona Day   Over You

"I need to go shopping for personal items," I said.

"Not today. You need to go get X-rays and I have things to handle," he said.

"I need to get some clothes," I said agitated. I was getting to the point where I was sick of his demands. If he wanted me to do this for him, he needed to be a little more considerate.

"I'll have Sandy choose some clothes for you and send them over. Are you ready?" he asked. Now, he was getting me riled which was like a baby pushing over a semi. I never let anger get to me. I wasn't angry now but just frustrated with his lack of compassion.

"Are we at least going to discuss what happened earlier? And how long I'm going to be staying here?" I asked. "I have an apartment back in Dothan full of my belongings, Jarvis. I just can't abandon my life."

He walked over to me and tilted my chin up, so I was looking him in the eyes.

"We fucked. We're going to be fucking a lot while you're here. Don't make a big deal about it," he said. He smacked me on the ass. "Yo shit will be fine until this is over." He walked out the bedroom.

I had to be out of my mind to agree to this stupidity, but here I was getting in the back of a limo driven by a tall, bulky, black guy that I assumed was Bahka.

After my tests were cleared at the doctor's office, we went back to Jarvis' house. I closed myself up in the bedroom trying to understand why I was there and asking myself why I wanted to be there. I only saw Jarvis when I came down to eat dinner. He didn't say a signal word to me until he informed me that he was leaving for a business trip.

Two Days Later

Jarvis

*W*hen I walked inside my bedroom, Nova jumped off the bed in a fit of rage with nothing but my T-shirt on. She ranted about me mistreating her and leaving her here alone with no phone or clothes. The same way she was trapped in this house was the same way she'd been trapped in my head. She had no escape from my house, and I had no escape from her for two whole years.

"When you shut da fuck up, I'll take you to get your necessities," I said. "I know you wear ugly shit, so I bought you this until Sandy brings you some clothes to choose from."

"Amoy is right. You've lost your mind, Jarvis," she said. She grabbed the bag from my hand and stormed in the bathroom.

I went and sat in the living area of the bedroom. About ten minutes later, she came out of the bathroom and stood in front of me. The long, floral dress was ugly as hell, but her beauty made it look good.

"Thank you," she said with a smile. She had walked into the bathroom furious with me and walked out completely calm. Nova never let negativity control her. She used to talk about channeling her positive energy to push out the negative.

"Let's go," I said, standing up.

She picked the worse time to go shopping. It was lunch time and the Atlanta traffic was at a complete stop. Thinking about how good her pussy felt strangling my dick for the two minutes I lasted made my dick start to harden as we sat in traffic. I could hardly concentrate on my business trip for thinking about how good she felt. All I could do was call her name like a whipped dog begging for mercy. If Amoy wouldn't have walked in on us, my bitch ass probably would've been in the fetal position crying like a newborn. That's just how good she felt. My dick started telling my mouth how good she felt, and my mouth started to water. I glanced at her and caught her staring at my hard dick that was bunched up in my trousers. Raising a brow at her made her blush and look away. Looking straight ahead, I raised the partition, reached down and slid my hand under her dress. *No panties.*

"I'm bout to eat your pussy," I said looking straight ahead. Sliding one finger between her legs, I felt her pussy jump and start to lubricate my finger. She slowly started to gyrate her hips against my finger as it slid up and down. I leaned over and nibbled on her earlobe.

"Sit across from me," I said ready to devour the sweet aroma coming from her. She took off the flat, black shoes I had bought her and sat across from me. I watched as she pulled the dress over her head and spread her legs wide while staring at me. Her clean-shaven glistening pussy lips were fat and enticing. She surprised me when she lifted her legs placing the soles of her feet on the seat. That made me realize Nova had been wanting this as much as I had. We were going to fuck each other until this shit was out both our systems.

The thought of having her anywhere, anytime and whenever made my dick throb. She stroked her middle finger between her pussy lips and started fingering herself. This wasn't the way this shit was supposed to go, but I was stuck watching her. I leaned forward ready to taste the sweet aroma that filled the back of the limo. Nova stopped me in my tracks by gently placing the sole of her left foot against my chest. She winked at me and continued to pleasure herself. Nova wanted me to see how sexy and alluring she was. I was captivated by her performance and thirsty to taste her. With her foot still in my chest, I started licking and sucking her toes. Never in my life had I ever thought of sucking a woman's toes, but Nova wasn't just any woman. She was my sexual being. The way she moaned my name while winding her hips and finger fucking herself caused my mouth to fill with saliva. Her moans got louder as she neared her orgasm. She finally removed her foot from my chest.

"Come with me," she moaned as she neared her orgasm.

I pulled my dick from my trousers and started jacking off with my eyes still glued to her. The splashing sounds of her pleasing herself were causing my dick to throb in my hand. The closer she came to coming, the harder I jacked my dick. Precum oozed out and I was grunting like a cave man from watching the show she was giving me. My nut sack was tight and full. When she finally came, my dick shot off so hard my cum almost hit the roof of the limo. Her juices sprayed out like a fire truck hose. I'm not talking metaphorically. I mean her sparkling fluid splattered all over me.

Nona Day   Over You

Even though I had just launched a load, my shit was still hard. I reached over and yanked her up from the seat making her straddle my lap. She stuck her wet fingers in my mouth allowing me to sample her flavor before replacing them with her tongue. Gripping her waist, I slammed her down on my dick. Nova's body shook like an 8.0 earthquake, releasing another liquifying orgasm. She cried out in painful pleasure. Throwing her head back, she enjoyed my mouth on her breasts. Just being inside her was a feeling like no other. Her walls were contracting around my shaft. She held her head up and pulled my face from her breast forcing me to look at her intoxicated eyes.

"I feel your heartbeat inside of me," she said. She wasn't lying. My heartbeat was in sync with the pounding in my shaft. Once again, all I could do was call her name. Nova started rocking her hips back and forth causing my dick to slide in and out of her. I reached down and grabbed her ass cheeks causing her pussy to allow me to bury myself deeper inside her.

"Aaaahhh Jaaarviiss!" she cried out my name.

"Keep coming on this dick, Nova!" I pleaded with her.

Her eyes rolled in the back of her head as her body shivered. I didn't stop. My dick was learning every sensitive spot inside of her. She started coming back to back. I shot off a load and started bouncing her up and down on me.

"Fuuuucckkk!" I roared. She had put a death grip on my dick as her orgasm ripped through her. I looked down to see my dick coated with a thick, milky cream. Her sweaty body was glistening, and tears flowed down her face as I continued burying my myself in her.

Nova was too intoxicated to help me push this last nut out, so I wrapped my arms around her waist. She fell into my chest with her face snuggled against my neck, whispering in my ear about how good I felt inside her I jack hammered my dick inside of her until I came so hard my stomach cramped up.

"Gah-damn! Nova, you gotta get up. I gotta serious ass cramp in my stomach," I said. She moved from my lap as quickly as her drained body would let her. I leaned forward trying to ease the pain.

"No, lean back," she said, pulling at my shoulders. I did as she said, and she started massaging my abs. It took a minute, but the pain slowly started to diminish.

"Better?" she asked smiling up at me.

"Yea," I replied, sitting up.

"Guess there's no shopping for me today," she said sadly. There was no way we could go in the stores. Sex oozed from our pores and I was soaked with her essence from my waist to my thighs.

"We can go home, have some lunch and come back later," I suggested.

"I don't even have anything to wear back later," she said.

"I'll have some things delivered to the house before we come back out," I told her. She started to get dressed.

I turned on the intercom. "What da fuck going on, Bahka? We been in traffic for over an hour."

"Not exactly. I just been riding around enjoying the scenery," he said. I couldn't see him, but I felt the silly ass grin on his face. Between Nova's moans and my groans, it was obvious what was going on.

A Few Hours Later

When we got back to the house, we showered together. I couldn't keep my hands off her, so I fucked her against the shower wall. Sandy came over with more than enough clothes. Nova disapproved of everything, except a few jogging sets. Today she chose to wear a white and black Puma jogging set and Puma sneakers. Nova had gained a couple of pounds, because her ass was looking plump. It was barely a handful, but it was enough. She sat in the passenger seat of my white Tesla. I felt her eyes on me as I drove.

"What?" I asked.

"You're not complaining about my music. You hate neo-soul and acoustic music," she said. I had become accustomed to listening to the music, because it reminded me of her. Eventually I found myself soaking in every lyric to the songs. I still didn't like the music, but the words spoke to me.

"I still don't like it," I replied. She laughed. There was something about seeing her happy in my presence that warmed my heart. She looked out the window and my hand found its way between her thighs.

She looked over at me. "I heard on the radio that you were getting married. Congratulations, but why aren't you on your honeymoon?

"I didn't get married," I said bluntly.

"Why didn't you get married, Jarvis," she asked shocked.

"Because I have unresolved issues with you that I'm trying to fix now," I answered honestly.

"And you think having sex with me is going to resolve them?" she asked. "I'm not the issue, Jarvis. You are."

I slammed on the brakes harder than I realized, but I hated when she didn't wear her seatbelt. We argued about it many times she had rode with me. We were lucky the airbags didn't pop out. Her head almost hit the dashboard.

"Put on yo gah-damn seatbelt, Nova," I demanded. "That's why yo lil ass got thrown out that damn matchbox."

She jerked the seatbelt and snapped it across herself angrily. She looked cute as hell with her pouty face that matched her lips.

"Now, tell me how I'm the issue," I said, calming my voice.

"Nothing Jarvis. Just drive, so we can get this day over," she said never looking my way. She was already getting tired of me. Nova brought the old me out. The me that I kept hidden from everyone else. She was the one person I thought I could be myself around. I couldn't push her away this soon. Not with the hold she had on me. I gently grabbed her chin forcing her to face me. It ached my heart to see the tears in her eyes.

"What da hell you crying for?" I asked.

"I haven't meditated in a couple of days. I'm just feeling off balance," she explained. One tear slid down her cheek. Placing my hand on the side of her face, I wiped the tear away with my thumb.

"I'm sorry for snapping at you," I said surprising myself. A big smile spread across her face.

"That's the first time you've ever apologized for being mean to me. And you've been mean plenty of times," she said.

"I'm only mean to people I like," I said surprising myself again. She blushed.

"Do you like me enough to take me shopping at some thrift stores?" she asked.

"No," I answered bluntly.

All eyes were on us when we stepped out of the car. Nova was so in her feelings she didn't notice everyone staring at us. I didn't come to my old stomping grounds in Atlanta that often anymore, but I made sure to give back abundantly. Nova grabbed a shopping basket and started throwing all her necessities inside of it. When that one was full, she passed it to me and grabbed another. By the time we left the store, Nova had three baskets full of voodoo equipment.

"You wanna grab some ice cream or something?" I asked when we got back in the car. It was an effort to put a smile on her face again.

"No thank you. I just wanna go back to the house," she said dryly.

Instead of driving toward the house, I went in the opposite direction. Nova sat quietly not asking any questions until we parked in front of an animal shelter.

"Dropping me off with the abandoned animals?" she asked sarcastically. I couldn't help but laugh out loud, because Nova's mouth was always witty.

"Just get out the car, Nova," I said. She walked beside me toward the store. To ease the tension between us, I gently grabbed her hand and folded my fingers between hers. She looked up giving me that smile again.

When we entered the shelter, I told her to pick out a puppy. I only had a few more days to spend day and night with her before I got back on the grind. She'd need someone to keep her company. We went in different directions looking at the animals.

"Hell nah, Nova! I said pick out a dog not that evil ass looking cat," I said as she came walking toward me with a black cat in her arms.

"Please Jarvis. Black cats are not evil. They're protectors. He's so beautiful," she pleaded with me. The damn cat was staring at me like he wanted to claw my eyes out.

"Nova, I don't like cats. And the way he's looking at me, he doesn't like me either," I explained. Her smile slowly started to leave her face.

"Keep da gah-damn cat. But it better not scratch up shit in my house!" I said angrily, walking toward the front of the shelter.

I carried the kennel to the car with Nova singing and dancing beside me. She was overly excited to have the furry, black cat. We ended up at Pet Smart buying all kinds of crap for her new pet.

"Thank you," she said. She leaned over and kissed me on the cheek as I drove back to the house.

I glanced back at the kennel. "What are you going to name it?"

"Binx," she said smiling. I chuckled and shook my head.

*****

I carried all the bags inside while Nova carried the kennel into the house. I demanded she put the kennel in the family room. No cat was going to be in my bedroom. I let her choose the room for her meditation. I didn't protest when she chose the living area of the master bedroom.

I helped her unpack the bags, asking questions about every crystal, candle, incense, oils and the other belongings she pulled from the bag. I told her she could use the canning room to make her herb blends. She usually grew her own herbs but had to settle for store bought items this time. After everything was done, I left her in the bedroom to do whatever she needed to do to get her emotions in check.

An hour later, Nova came walking through the house with burning sage. I had dealt with a couple of females that used it, so I didn't trip. I mainly didn't trip because she was butt ass naked. She could've set the house on fire and my eyes still would've been on her. When I told her she would have to walk around the house naked if she didn't pick out any clothes, she took it literally.

Later that night, we chilled in the theatre room smoking, laughing and talking like two years hadn't passed between us. Nova was goofy and funny, so she always kept me in good spirits.

"I just discovered the elevator in the house," she said as she sat next to me in the theater room.

"Yea, I never use it," I said. "Housekeeping uses it a lot."

"I'm not going to use it either," she said. "The steps gon' make this booty fat."

She stood up and started twerking making me laugh. I stopped laughing when she turned on the surround sound and started working her body. Nova did yoga, so she was flexible as fuck. My dick felt like it was going to break. I watched as long as I could before I had her legs pinned behind her head. She was so damn addictive.

After about an hour of sex, we were naked watching some cartoon movie she wanted to watch.

"Come with me," she said, reaching out for my hand. I gave her my hand and she led me upstairs to our bedroom. "Lay on the bed on your stomach."

"Ain't that kinda freak," I said, stepping back from her.

She laughed. "Just do it."

I gave her a side eye and did as she said. The lights in the bedroom went dim and she walked around lighting candles. Kem's voice started playing over the surround sound. I only knew his music because of Nova. She straddled my back.

"You always so tense," she said. I felt warm liquid dropping on my back. The sensual, soft touches of her hands rubbing the liquid on my back was soothing. Kneading, caressing, massaging and stroking her delicate hands from my neck down to the soles of my feet removed all the tension I had built up. I flipped over on my back to receive the same treatment.

She massaged my temples. "You are a remarkable man Jarvis Michael Alexandria. You're funny, protective, loyal and strong. A true king you are."

Her words touched my soul as I drifted off to sleep.

Next Morning

Nova was in the shower singing from the top of her longs along with Ari Lennox on the surround sound. Nova had a beautiful voice and made me smile to hear happiness in her voice. I didn't know what was going to happen between us, but I didn't see letting her go anytime soon. She gave me a peaceful happiness that I've yearned for a long time. As I made my way down to my office, the front doorbell rang. Rochelle was walking toward the door the same time as me.

"I got it, Rochelle," I said. She smiled, nodded her head and walked away. I opened the door.

"We have a crisis," she said, walking in without being invited.

Nona Day   Over You

"Wooaahh! Walk yo ass back out my damn door. I ain't invite yo ass in here," I told her. Deidra knew the old me, so she wasn't shocked by my rude mannerisms. She rolled her eyes and walked back to the other side of the door. I slammed it in her face and opened it again with a smile on my face.

"Really Jarvis?" she asked agitated.

"Now, you may enter," I said, stepping to the side. "Step in my study so we can talk."

She followed behind me. I took a seat on the sofa while she sat in the high back Queen style chair.

"What's the crisis?" I asked. She passed me the tablet. I scanned through pictures of Nova and me at the spiritual store and animal shelter. The blog talked about Nova practicing witchcraft and shit. I didn't consider this a crisis, but I understood what Deidra was getting at. The people in my circle were close minded. They liked people they could control with their money and power. Nova wasn't one of those people. Being associated with her could cause me to lose business.

"What you suggest?" I asked.

"Clean up her image ASAP," she suggested.

Nona Day   Over You

I laughed. "She's not me. Nova doesn't give a fuck about what people think about her. She's with me for me and no one else."

"People are talking, Jarvis. They even found out about you stopping the real estate project where her parents own a farm. That's not a good look for a young, up and coming tycoon like yourself," she warned me.

"I pay you to clean my image not hers. So do what da fuck needs to be done," I said.

"Get rid of her. I'm sure you eventually will, like you do every woman that finds herself in your bed," she said sarcastically.

I laughed. "You still mad I stopped fucking you?"

Before she could reply, Nova walked into the study with absolutely nothing on. The way Deidra stared with her mouth open was hysterical. Nova walked over and sat beside me on the sofa. She leaned over and kissed me on the lips. She must've been listening to the conversation in the hall. Feeling territorial, she walked in after discovering me and Deidra's previous relationship.

"Nova, this is Deidra, my image consultant," I said.

Nona Day   Over You

"Hi, nice to meet you. Will you be joining us for Jarvis' birthday dinner?" Nova asked Deidra with a smile.

Deidra finally closed her mouth to speak. Nova's whimsical nature made people think she was weak. She wasn't confrontational but she wouldn't let anyone push her over. Humble but firm. Soft spoken but bold and outspoken when need be. Her balance was on point. Instead of coming at Deidra's throat in a confrontational manner, she silenced her with wit.

"No," she said, standing up. "Jarvis, we'll discuss this later. Enjoy your birthday."

I caught up with Deidra as she opened her car door.

"You're becoming a powerful man, Jarvis. You want to have someone like that on your arm?"

"Get out yo damn feelings and do your gah-damn job. And if you ever try to utter a disrespectful word about her out of yo dick sucking, cum guzzling ass mouth, I will fuck yo entire world up," I said between gritted teeth.

"I-I wasn't trying to disrespect her," she said nervously.

"Well, you did!" I barked louder than I intended causing Deidra to jump.

"I'll do what I can to minimize the damage," she said.

"You don't seem to understand. She ain't no damn damage. If I didn't have her to come home to, I wouldn't be able to uphold this fake ass facade," I said. "Let whoever think what da fuck they want."

She stared at me. "You really do love her, don't you?"

"Not sure about that yet, but she ain't going anywhere anytime soon," I confessed.

She apologized for coming over unannounced and disrespecting Nova in anyway. I didn't apologize for my remarks because I meant every word. Nova was right to want no parts of my world. But I would burn this city down about her. When I walked in the house, Nova was standing by the banister nervous as hell.

"It's not nice to eavesdrop," I said, walking up to her.

"I'm sorry. I was bringing you your phone because Amoy called, but I overheard her talking about me," she said, holding out my phone. I took it and stepped backwards taking as many pictures of her as she would allow. When she sat on the step and opened her legs wide. My dick jumped; I moved in closer snapping pictures of my treasure chest.

A few minutes later, I sat beside her on the stairs. It was quiet between us for a few minutes. I didn't know how to tell Nova I wanted her in my life willingly after practically forcing her to be with me. She was only here because I wanted her here. I'm sure if I gave her the chance to leave, she would walk right out the front door without giving me a second thought. Even the good pipe I was laying on her wasn't enough to keep her here.

She laid her head on my shoulder. My entire body relaxed as she laced her fingers between mine.

"I don't wanna ruin your image. I'm going to start wearing the clothes Sandy bought me whenever I leave the house," she said. "Besides I don't go out often, so I can suffer through it when I do."

She looked at me with a smile making my heart glow.

"Guess I have been keeping you inside like a hostage or something," I said smiling.

"Yea, pretty much," she said nudging my shoulder with hers.

"You wanna stay here with me and see where this goes?" I asked boldly, holding my breath.

She smiled. "Yea."

"We'll start getting out more and having some fun," I said. She kissed me softly on the jaw.

Two Weeks Later

Nova

$\mathcal{I}$ still had no clue as to what Jarvis and I were doing, but I was loving every minute of it. Not even my menstrual cycle could keep him away from me. The sex between us was indescribable. The energy and heat between us were breathtaking. Just the brush of his flesh against mine would make my body shiver. We hadn't even experienced each other orally because we were so in awe of just sexing each other.

With the new cellphone Jarvis bought me, I talked to my parents but didn't inform them that I was in Atlanta. He even allowed me to go out for drinks with Amoy and Cache. I had a ball laughing, drinking and singing at a karaoke bar with them. They asked questions about our relationship, but I told them as little as possible. Mostly because I still didn't understand what we were doing.

I used Jarvis' study to do virtual work to save up some money, but I spent a lot of time in the enormous greenhouse he had installed for me. He even had grape orchids planted on the acres of his backyard. It made me wonder about my length of time here. The orchids wouldn't be ready until next summer. Jarvis was spoiling me with expensive gifts and clothes, but these things weren't the way to my heart.

While he was gone, I spent time exploring the mansion and getting acquainted with the staff. There were so many rooms in the mansion I got lost a couple of times. Even though there was an in-house pool, I couldn't wait for summer to enjoy the pool outside. Then I wondered if I would still be here. I was a simple girl living a fairytale dream, but something still felt off. My place in his life was confusing.

Tonight, I was starting to miss being with him. It was day three and he was still out of town on a business trip with Dak and Noble. Today made five days since we'd had sex because I was cleansing myself with a yoni egg I had made. I was starting to miss him so much I called his phone over twenty times, but still didn't get an answer. Worry made me call Amoy to see had she heard from Dak. She informed me she had talked to him earlier that day. I guess Jarvis wasn't missing me as much as I missed him. Every day I tried to remind myself that this was a temporary stay and not to get my feelings involved. There was no way that was possible, because my heart was in it a long time ago. Sadness started to set inside my spirit, so I did a quick prayer and meditated. After I was done, I climbed into bed and clicked off the lights making the room pitch black.

I didn't know what time it was or how long I had been asleep, but the hunger in his voice woke me up.

"Open up for me, Nova."

I opened my eyes, but the room was so dark I couldn't see him.

"Turn on the lights. I wanna see you," I said, turning over on my back. "I've been calling you all day. I thought something happened."

"I know. I can't talk to you while I'm away. That shit hurts in a way that can't be fixed when you're not near me."

I could feel how much he wanted me, so I spread my legs. He slid inside me with a low growl but didn't move. He laid his body on top of mine and nestled his face in my neck.

"I miss smelling you," he murmured. No movement inside of me or anything. He just laid there buried deep inside me until he fell asleep. I didn't mind one bit. Skin to skin was all I needed at this moment.

He woke up an hour later drilling inside of me like a cave man. His growls and grunts were like a wild animal. My body was flipped and tossed from one end of the bed to the other end. Legs were pinned and folded while I was in a world of cosmic bliss coming back to back until we collapsed together.

When I woke up the next afternoon, Jarvis was working in his home office. I walked over and straddled his lap smothering his handsome face with kisses before I slid my tongue in his mouth. He caressed my naked body while our tongues played in each other's mouths.

"Nova, you gotta start wearing clothes. I do have a staff," he said breaking our kiss.

"You said if I didn't like the clothes, I'd have to walk around naked. I don't like them, so I agreed to only wear them when we go out in public," I reminded him. "Today is Friday, so there's no staff. What are you doing home?"

He smiled and shook his head. "I know you've been bored in the house. Thought we could do something together until tonight."

SOUL Publications

I couldn't help the cheesy grin that spread across my face. Enjoying a romantic day filled with fun with him would be nice. Most of our time together was spent sexing each other.

"What's tonight?" I asked

"We're attending a Chamber of Commerce dinner," he said.

I stood up from his lap.

"Jarvis I don't have enough time to get ready for that. Look at my hair, nails, toes and brows," I said.

"You got the entire day to get ready, so get on it," he said. "We agreed to get out and have some fun, so this our chance," he said

"Ok, but I don't let anyone touch my hair but my mom," I said. "I'm going to go let her do it and then I'll go get a mani and pedi," I said. "I can do my own brows."

"Nova, I have enough money to get your brows done," he said.

I laughed. "I know, but I like doing them myself."

I walked over and kissed him on the lips. "Pick out a dress you want me to wear tonight while I'm out."

Nona Day   Over You

After slipping on a Nike jogging suit, I called Bahka to pull the car to the front of the house. I was excited about enjoying a night out with Jarvis. This would be the first event I attended with him.

McDonough, GA

Daddy and Ma were ecstatic about my surprise visit. After shampooing and conditioning my hair, I let her blow it out and flat iron it for me. She asked me several questions about my retreat and job. I told so many lies it was downright shameful. I just wasn't ready to tell her I failed at committing to a stable career. She wanted so desperately for me to decide what I wanted to do with my life. It's not that I didn't want to work. My problem was I didn't want to work a job where it consumed me. I didn't want my ambition to be making millions. As long as I had enough money to live comfortably I was happy. Making millions wasn't a necessity for me. Tying myself to a job filled with stress, frustration and sleepless nights wasn't for me. Money changes people and makes them do things that they normally wouldn't do. It was my goal to never become one of those people. There was nothing wrong with having ambition and achieving a level of success to live comfortably, but so many will do anything for money. Life was meant to be enjoyed, not slaving yourself to the point you never get to enjoy the millions you made.

Daddy was so happy to see me, he stopped working in the farm to relax with me while Ma cooked. We watched old westerns while he drank a surprisingly expensive whiskey that I'd seen Jarvis drink. I guess the olive business along with his other produce was making him big bucks.

Just as Ma called us into the kitchen, someone rang the doorbell.

"Go ahead. I'll get it," Daddy said. I went into the kitchen and helped Ma prepare the table.

"Look who showed up for dinner," Daddy said happily. The plate in my hand crashed to the floor shattering into pieces.

"Jarvis?" I asked as if it couldn't possibly be him. Bahka must've told him where he took me.

"You two know each other?" Ma asked, walking up to Jarvis giving him a warm, inviting hug. He looked at me over her head and winked.

Nona Day   Over You

"Yea, we're old friends. Didn't know Nova was your daughter though," he lied. And it was a big, bold faced lie.

"H-How do you know my parents?" I asked anxiously.

"Jarvis saved this rural area from turning into malls and condos. Some big shot real estate developer tried pushing us out until Jarvis here stepped in. He even helped me get the olive fields started. Ain't that something. Fine young man here," Daddy said, patting him on the back. Jarvis smiled and winked at me. To hide my smile I quickly bent down to pick up the shattered plate.

Daddy and Ma acted like I didn't exist at the dinner table. Jarvis had their undivided attention. He was the charismatic, dignified, gentleman with them. He talked eloquently and had better table manners than the richest of the rich. I didn't know who this man was talking to my parents. He looked like Jarvis but that wasn't *my* Jarvis.

"Nova should attend one of those commerce dinners to network with the big wigs. That way she can move back closer to us," Ma suggested. "She's doing so good at her job I'm sure they'll give her an outstanding reference. They let her use the company limo with a chauffeur just to surprise us for a day."

"Oh is that right?" Jarvis asked staring at me. I quickly looked away. Now I was the big, bold faced liar. I had told my parents I was here for a job convention this weekend. It was a relief when Daddy started talking about sports.

The remainder of the dinner was relaxed. I faded in the background while everyone talked. After dinner, Jarvis and Daddy went into the den to enjoy a slice of Ma's chocolate cake. I helped Ma clean up the kitchen before joining the men in the den.

"I better get going. I have to dress for this dinner party," Jarvis said, standing up. "Nova, would you care to accompany me?"

"That would be a fabulous idea," Ma answered for me.

"Sure Jarvis, I would love to be your date if you don't already have a date,", I replied jokingly.

He smiled and nodded his head.

"Nova, why don't you walk him out. I drank a lil too much of that expensive whiskey," Daddy said. Now, I knew where he got the whiskey from. *Jarvis.*

Nona Day   Over You

We walked to his black Audi in silence. He leaned against the door and wrapped his arms around my waist pulling me into him.

"You didn't have to do that to your hair. I like it nappy," he said smiling at me.

"I know, but I want to represent you well,"," I replied.

"Thank you," I said breaking our kiss.

"For what?" He asked.

"For saving my parents' farm," I replied.

"You're welcome. Now go tell your parents I'm dropping you off at the imaginary hotel you are staying at," he said with a big grin.

"Hush," I said jokingly

Before we left, I grabbed a couple of crates of wine I had made on my last visit home. When we got back to the house, Jarvis wanted a quickie, but I couldn't. The way we sexed each other my roots would swell up and ruin my bone straight hair.

*****

After I got dressed in the dress Jarvis chose for me, I made my way down the stairs where Jarvis was waiting for me. I had gotten used to seeing him in suits but tonight he looked like an Egyptian God in his tuxedo. He had a beautiful fur coat thrown over his arm. I hated to disappoint him, but I wasn't wearing that coat.

"Jarvis, thank you, but I can't wear animal fur."

"It's a damn chinchilla. This coat cost me thirty-five thousand dollars. You gon' wear this damn coat, Nova," he said angrily.

"I didn't ask you to buy me that coat. I'm not wearing it," I stated firmly but softly.

"Don't yo ass eat chickens and turkey. Them damn animals. I've even seen yo ass wearing a damn shirt that looked like you skinned big bird to make it," he said frustrated.

I couldn't help but laugh. "Food not fashion. And those feathers on my shirt were fake."

"Fuck it! I'll give it to Rochelle," he said referring to his top housekeeper.

"No, we can return it for a nice cashmere coat." I tried bargaining to calm him down.

"You better be glad yo pussy good," he said, throwing the coat over the banister.

"Wait til you experience my mouth," I said, winking at him..

He threw me over his shoulder like I was a feather. "Fuck that party."

I had to beg and plead for him to put me down. I wanted to go out and enjoy an evening with him.

Commerce Dinner

I thought the long, black cocktail dress I wore would make Jarvis drool, but he didn't seem impressed. He told me he didn't give a damn about the dress only what was under it. Said my beauty surpassed any piece of clothing. That made me love him more.

I was so relieved to see Amoy and Cache at the dinner. We talked about all the stuffy, rich folks as we sipped on wine. I was glad I ate at my parents' house, because the thousand-dollar meals didn't look appetizing. I watched

Jarvis interact with some of the most prominent people of Atlanta. He was in a zone and I was mesmerized by the man he had become. Cache and Amoy walked around talking with people they knew. Since I didn't know anyone there, I sat observing everyone before making my way to the ladies' room.

After relieving myself, I was washing my hands when a brown-skinned beauty with an exquisite dress on walked inside. She smiled at me as she walked toward me. I immediately felt the bad vibes coming from her.

"Hi, I'm Valentine, Jarvis' ex-fiancé. Are you Nova?" she asked. I didn't know how to feel about meeting her, because I somewhat felt guilty for ruining her wedding.

"Yes, I am," I answered.

"Enjoy whatever time he gives you. I'm giving him time to get whatever this thing is he has for you out of his system. I hope you're not in it for love. Get all the gifts, sex and money you can. Leave your heart out of it," she said before walking out, leaving me filled with so much doubt.

I made my way out of the restroom and find Jarvis conversing with a couple of white men and a black man, so

I made my way over to him. He gently slid his hand around my waist and introduced me to everyone.

"You wasted no time replacing Valentine," Carl, the black man said with a smile with his eyes roaming over my body. Jarvis' grip around my waist became tighter.

"Respect," Jarvis said between gritted teeth, staring at Carl. I felt the rage building inside him. I looked up and gave him a smile, letting him know I could handle it.

"What's your career field, young lady," Phillip, the older white man asked. "You've got to have goals to be with a man of this caliber. Hope you're not one of those Instagram influencer like so many young women are choosing to become these days."

It was my time to get heated. These men were chauvinistic buttholes.

"Have you been scoping those women out on Instagram?" I asked. "I wouldn't think a man of your age and sophistication would know anything about Instagram models."

He looked like the type to pay for cheap call girls.

"Hey, can't blame a man for enjoying eye candy if it's on display," he replied.

"What do you do?" Chris, the younger white guy asked. He looked no more than twenty-five."

"I'm a virtual assistant," I answered.

"Nova also has her master's degree," Jarvis said. "She's just taking her time to choose the right job."

"Well, she's got the right man to help her do that," Phillip said. "He knows what it's like to come from living the rough life. He left the street life to join teams of real men trying to accomplish goals. It's very few black man that have achieved goals like Jarvis and Carl here. Wish we had more like them. They're fine examples of young, black men that doesn't want to blame America and slavery for their failures."

"We donate so much to the black communities and get no kind of gratitude for our kind acts," Chris said.

"Is that why you do it?" I asked. "For recognition from the poor, black folks?"

The two white men looked at me as if I was speaking foreign language. It was obvious they weren't used to a black person questioning them. Carl dropped his head.

"Are you ready to go," Jarvis asked nearly cutting off my circulation around my waist. My ribs were going to be sore in the morning from the tight hold he had on me.

"Please," I said, quickly. I wanted this to be a night of fun and getting to know his colleagues and business associates, but it wasn't any fun. This was an evening of uppity, privilege, rich folks judging each other and talking down on people they know nothing about.

The ride home was quiet with me deep in my thoughts. I knew things between us started out as a temporary, dysfunctional relationship but we'd grown closer. Well, we'd grown closer physically and sexually but emotionally and mentally we were still distant in our relationship. And I still had no clue as to what we were doing.

"You gon' tell me what's bothering you or you gon' look crazy as hell the rest of the night?" Jarvis asked as we rode in the back of the limo. The long split in my dress allowed him to place his hand between my thighs like always.

"How do you deal with those people?" I asked.

"It's what I have to do. It's not easy, but it's necessary Nova," he tried explaining. There wasn't enough money in the world that would force me to be around that kind of energy.

"Sorry if I made your friends uncomfortable," I said.

"It's fine Nova," he said. "It's something you'll get used to dealing with." *Never.*

"At least everyone wasn't bad. I did meet a few nice people," I said. "I met your ex-fiancé tonight. She's beautiful," I said nervously.

"So what? So are you," he said.

"I kind of felt guilty knowing I'm the reason you didn't marry her," I confessed.

"You ain't the reason, Nova. I am. Ain't that what you said?" he asked angrily. "What da fuck she say to you?"

"Nothing, she just introduced herself," I lied. I didn't want to repeat her words, because I didn't want him to confirm what she said to me.

"Come here, Nova," he said, patting his lap. The long split in my dress allowed me to straddle his lap.

"What she say?" he asked again pinning my hair behind my ears. "And don't say nothing."

"She said you were going to use me up and throw me away. It hurts because I know she's right," I said getting teary eyed. "I'm not mad because you told me that from the start, but it still hurts to hear someone else say it."

He pulled my face toward his and kissed me softly.

"Are you happy with me, Nova?" he asked. I nodded my head. "Then fuck what she say."

Those were not comforting or assuring words, but I let it go. I decided at that moment to just take advantage of every moment with him. I looked at my phone and it was after midnight.

"Happy Birthday," I said smiling at him.

"Damn, you remember?" he asked shocked.

"Of course I do, and you better remember mine," I said, rolling my eyes at him.

He laughed. "July 4th."

Nona Day   Over You

All I could do was smile. When we made it home, there was no sex. We stripped out of our clothes and cuddled until we fell asleep.

Jarvis

I woke to Nova straddling my lap with her wild straight hair and big beautiful smile. She was simply perfection. Leaning forward she kissed my lip softly before finding her way to my neck.

"I'm going to make you a cake for your birthday but first I'm going to taste you." She licked her way down my chest.

I'd had my dick sucked by bitches with no tonsils but the thought of Nova deep throating me freaked me out. My head was already fucked up over her pussy. If her mouth felt better, I was going to be hollering like a bitch. Her hair tickled my flesh as she made her way down low. I started finger combing her hair pulling it up into a ponytail like I was a five-star hair stylist.

She stopped and looked up at me. I became hypnotized by the lust in her eyes. Our eyes stayed locked on each other. Like always, she pulled me into a hypnotic state just by the look in her eyes. She licked her lips as she massaged my brick hard dick with her soft hand. Holding it with a firm grip, she stroked it up and down delicately. Her sweet saliva dropped from her mouth to the dome of my dick. When she twirled her tongue over my crown, I bit down on my bottom lip to hold in the groan.

Her tongue started stroking up, down and around my dome and shaft. She hadn't even taken me inside her mouth and saliva was dripping down to my nuts. That's just how wet her mouth was. Inch by inch she started sliding my shaft into her mouth, sucking and slurping more and more with each stroke. Her mouth was like a wet vacuum as she pulled me in and out of her mouth. My legs trembled and my abs tightened. I was fighting so hard to keep control, but she was making it impossible. Our eyes were still fucking each other while she performed magic on my dick. She buried me inside her mouth with her lips resting on the base. I felt her throat relax and my dome went deeper. She held it there, moaning loud and sending strong vibrations through my body.

"Aaaarrrgh!" I roared as I gripped her hair tighter and gently pulled her mouth off my dick. I couldn't take what she was doing to me.

"I wanna taste you," she murmured with saliva dripping from her chin.

Nona Day   Over You

She dipped down sucking my balls into her mouth. Her tongue twirled around my cum filled nut sack gently sucking them into her mouth. Precum oozed from my dome and my legs wouldn't stop shaking. I couldn't help but groan and call her name.

"Make love to my mouth," she murmured before placing my dick back in her mouth. I held on to her hair as I started thrusting my hips. She held her mouth open allowing me to ram my head against her throat. Tears started to slide down her face. She gagged as saliva flowed from her mouth. I felt tingly feelings in my toes as they curled up. My abs tightened as I started thrusting harder and faster. She pulled me into her eyes again. The room started to spin, and I saw flashing lights.

"Gah-damn, your mouth feels so damn good! Ssssssshhhit, Nova, I'm bout to come!" I roared. She gently massaged my balls while playing around with that sensitive area under my nuts causing me to lose all control as I erupted inside her mouth. She gripped my shaft and started pumping my cum from my dick into her mouth as she moaned draining me of my fluids. My entire body jerked and twitched with my mouth wide open. Every nerve in me was on alert. I felt as if I was going to combust, but I couldn't stop her. I had never felt such intense pleasure in my life. She finally released me. She looked up at me with watery eyes.

"You're so much sweeter than I thought."

All I could do was lay my head back and stare up at the ceiling. My body was floating in a universe full of bright stars. She laid her body on top of mine and I wrapped my arms around her.

"What the hell you doing to me?" I asked.

She kissed my chest. "Happy Birthday."

Nova climbed out of bed, and I could hear the shower come on. I wanted to join her, but I felt like an addict that had just stuck a needle in his arm. I was still ascended in air. By the time I came back down to reality, Nova had made her way downstairs. I took a shower and slipped on some jeans and a T-shirt.

When I walked in the kitchen, she had a mess all over the kitchen isle. Pots, pans and bowls were everywhere. Like always, she was as naked as the day she was born. Today was Sunday, so everyone was off, allowing her to walk around as she pleased.

Nona Day   Over You

"Do you know what you doing?" I asked standing on the other side of the kitchen isle. By the way she was holding the mixer, she didn't look experienced at baking a cake.

"Of course. I've watched Ma bake cakes plenty of times. I got this," she said smiling at me. She started vigorously stirring the ingredients in the bowl with a big wooden spoon until she was exhausted.

"It's not mixed well enough," she said, tasting the batter on her finger.

I watched as she put the cake mixer together. My heart and stomach fluttered at the love I had for her. This wasn't the plan. She wasn't supposed to come back into my life, fuck me up and make it to where I couldn't imagine life without her. The thought of not having her with me didn't sit well with me.

"I love you," I blurted out just as she turned on the mixer and stuck it in the bowl. She yelped when cake batter splattered everywhere. It was all over her face, breasts and the counter. I laughed hysterically and she stood there with her mouth open. She was truly a beautiful calamity.

"I'm sorry. I'll clean it up," she said looking at me sadly.

"I think you were supposed to put the mixer inside the batter before you turned it on," I told her as I walked to her. She turned around to face me.

"You knew I was going to make a mess," she said sadly.

"Nah, I was thinking about how much I love yo weird ass," I said with my heart pounding. I honestly didn't know how Nova felt about me loving her.

Her eyes widened as she looked up at me. "You mean me or my sex."

"I mean you, Nova."

She threw her batter covered arms around my neck. "I love you too. I love you so much, Jarvis."

She had turned me into a soft ass nigga. To hear her say those words brought tears to my heart. I held her tight as I closed my eyes to keep from shedding a tear.

"I'm going to clean up this mess and take you out for brunch. I'll just buy you a cake," she said, turning around to face the counter.

Nona Day   Over You

"What about all the cake batter on you?" I asked, kissing my way down her back. She looked over her shoulder.

"Ain't no cake batter back there," she said.

"Not yet. Now bend over," I replied. I grabbed the bowl and set it on the floor as I dropped to my knees.

Nova spread her legs and bent over the counter ready for me to indulge in eating her sweet pussy. I sucked her juicy lips inside my mouth before sliding my tongue between them. The melody of my name coming from her made my dick grow. Dipping my finger in the cake batter mix, I spread it between her folds. Feasting on her sweet pussy was like a drug. The more I did it, the more I wanted. I flicked my tongue against her swollen clit until she moaned loudly in ecstasy as she gushed out her sweetness all over me like a fire hydrant. I tried to drink every single drop. Her legs gave way after she came, and I held her by the waist to keep her from falling.

"Get on the counter and put that ass in the air," I said, smacking her ass. She got on the kitchen isle on all fours. I grabbed the bowl off the floor, separated her ass cheeks and spread cake batter between them. Grabbing one of the stools, I took a seat positioning myself for a sweet treat. My tongue lapped between her cheeks devouring the batter before tongue fucking her ass. With two fingers inserted inside her drenched pussy, Nova was trying to run while her sweet fluid cascaded all over the counter. I wrapped my arms around her thighs to keep her from running. My tongue stroked from her pussy to her ass. Her clit was swollen as hard as my dick when I sucked it into my mouth. She cried out her love for me before baptizing me. My dick shot off a load just from hearing the agonizing pleasure in her voice. Her body shivered uncontrollably when I was done with her.

I carried her limp body upstairs and laid her across the bed until I ran her a bath. About twenty minutes later, I had her relaxed in the tub with her back against my chest. I didn't care about sharing her with the world. Being closed up in the house with her was all I wanted for my birthday. She decided to leave the baking alone and just cook us dinner. That was good with me, because I knew she could cook.

Later that evening, we went to Amoy and Dak's house. When we arrived, everyone close to me was there. I had the happiest birthday I'd had in two years.

Two Months Later

Nova

*T*he holidays had come and gone. We spent Thanksgiving with my parents and enjoyed Christmas and New Years with Amoy and everyone else. Jarvis bought me a brand-new Audi coupe for Christmas. I would've settled for a piece of junk, but he insisted. With him being a man that had everything, I had no idea what to get him, and me not having much money made it hard to buy him anything. I settled for finally agreeing to wear the closet full of clothes Sandy had picked out for me. None of the clothes fit my style, but I decided it was the least I could do.

Jarvis was out of town again for his January annual company conference. He asked me to come with him, but I declined. Amoy and Cache had come over to keep me company.

"You look weird in coordinated clothing," Cache said smiling at me. "I mean I like the outfit, but I'm not used to seeing you dressed in subtle colors that meshed well together."

"I agree to wear the clothes Sandy chose for me," I said. "The clothes are beautiful. I just gotta get used to them."

"Are you okay Nova?" Amoy asked. "Is he forcing you to wear these clothes?"

"Only when we go out in public," I said. "When we're here alone, I'm naked."

They laughed thinking I was joking.

"Well, don't change who you are for him or anyone else." Amoy said.

"I won't," I said smiling at her.

"Where's Binx?" Amoy asked as we sat in the den sipping on wine.

"Probably upstairs curled up in the bed. He tries to beat Jarvis to the bed. Jarvis will wake me up to make Binx get out the bed. He's so scared of my cat," I said laughing.

"Girl, I swear you need to market this damn wine. Half a glass and I'm feeling it," Cache said.

"She needs to market everything she makes: herb blends, wine, hair and health care products," Amoy suggested. "You have your own little fortune right in the canning room and don't know it."

It had been hard enough trying to stay lowkey from blogs trying to get a story on the new "temporary" woman in Jarvis' bed. It bothered bloggers that they knew little to nothing about me. The last thing I wanted to do was draw attention to myself. But I couldn't say I hadn't been thinking about selling my products. Then the thought of all the work I would have to put in pushed the thought out of my mind. Starting a business from the ground up was time consuming and stressful.

Then again, I thought of how proud Ma would be. I finally confessed and told her I had moved back home and was living with Jarvis but made sure to leave out how I ended up back with him. They weren't pleased with me shacking up with a man. My parents were old school but respected the fact that I was grown enough to make my own decisions. Regardless of how rich Jarvis was, Ma wanted me to have a career.

"I wouldn't know where to start?" I admitted.

"Start with a name for your business. We can figure all that out," Amoy suggested.

"I'll make you a business Facebook page. That'll help get your products out there," Cache added. I sat silently and considered everything they said and wondering if I could really do this.

"Ok! Let's do it!" I jumped and shouted. Amoy and Cache jumped excitedly with cheers for my new adventure.

"We gotta go out and celebrate," Cache said, twerking all that behind she was carrying. I laughed.

Amoy and I hollered at the same time, "Strip club!"

I loved climbing stripper poles. Practicing yoga for so many years made my body quite limber. Then I realized I couldn't be out there climbing poles. That was not the image I needed as Jarvis' girlfriend or starting a business. I didn't want to do anything to cause an argument between us when he got home. Jarvis would drink and smoke himself into a slumber after every trip. I tried forcing him to talk to me about it, but we would end up arguing. Eventually, I stopped trying. Confrontations are not for me.

We all agreed to go to Dak's club and chill in the VIP. Since I didn't have anything to wear, we hit up a mall.

When I got back to the house to get dressed, I tried calling Jarvis. He never answered my calls when he was out of town on business trips.

Jarvis wouldn't approve of the dress Amoy and Cache picked out for me, but I loved it. I hadn't worn anything I wanted since I'd been with Jarvis. It felt liberating to shop for myself. The short, shimmery, backless dress fit my body perfectly. I didn't know if it was the sex, but my butt was getting bigger. I twerked in the long mirror to watch it bounce, making me giggle to myself. My hair was back to its natural, curly, untamable self.

*****

When I saw Bahka calling my phone, I grabbed my lip gloss and phone. Cache and I smoked a blunt on the way to the club, and Amoy sipped on more of my wine. The line to get inside was wrapped around the building, so Bahka escorted us to the front of the club. Amoy had a VIP table of course. It was filled with expensive wine and liquor. It only took a couple of hours before we were having the time of our life. We didn't get on the dance floor because our little private section was popping enough for us. Laughing and enjoying being free tonight made me realize how much I missed it.

"Oh shit!" Cache said, sitting down with her eyes glued to the VIP entrance. My heart skipped at least two beats when I saw the anger in Jarvis' eyes. I couldn't move as he approached us. The closer he got, I knew he was either drunk or high by his low red eyes…if not both.

"Let's go," he said staring at me.

"She's just having fun, Jarvis. We'll make sure she gets home safe," Amoy said trying to defend me.

"Shut da fuck up and stay da fuck outta this," he said staring at Amoy. "Now get up."

It was rare to see this side of Jarvis out in public. I knew to get up because this was the old Jarvis staring at me. It wasn't that I was worried about him hurting me because he would never do such a thing, but there was no telling what he would do to anyone that even stepped on his shoe right now. He was walking so fast to get out of the club, I couldn't keep up. When I stepped outside, some guy ran his stupid mouth. Jarvis was only standing a few feet away from me, but I was sure he didn't know who I was to Jarvis.

"Damn, that ass looking fat as hell in that dress. I bet that dark chocolate pussy good as fuck. They say black bitches got the best."

I immediately jumped in front of Jarvis when he turned around. My skinny behind stood no chance at holding him back. He kept walking me backwards with his eyes on his prey until my back was against the guy. Jarvis lifted me up like a piece of paper and moved me to the side.

"What da fuck you just say to her?" he asked the guy. The guy looked like he was going to pee or mess on his self; he was so scared. Everyone in eye or ear distance clammed up. It was like I could hear a pin drop.

"Shit Jarhead, ain't know that was you. My bad," he answered with a tremble in his voice.

"Now greet her as mine," Jarvis demanded.

The terrified boy gave me his attention. "I'm sorry for being disrespectful, Queen. You deserve to be treated with the utmost respect just for being a beautiful, black woman. You are the mother of all life. Please except my apologies."

"It's okay," I said. I wanted to quickly deescalate this situation and go home.

"Now, kiss her feet," Jarvis said.

"Jarvis, stop it. He doesn't have to do that. That's dehumanizing," I said feeling totally sorry for the guy.

"Ain't what da fuck he said to you dehumanizing?" Jarvis asked with his eyes still glued to the guy. The guy started to bend down to do as he was ordered, but Jarvis stopped him. I breathed a huge sigh of relief. "Yo mouth ain't worthy to touch her. Now, get da fuck out my face."

We got in the backseat and Bahka drove. Jarvis was seething with so much anger I could smell it along with the stench of Bourbon. He cussed Bahka out for bringing me to the club, and Bahka argued back with him. They didn't seem like boss and employer, but the relationship worked for them. I made a mental note to apologize to Bahka for dragging him into this mess. The partition went back up after he was done.

"We weren't doing anything but having fun," I tried explaining.

"Shut da fuck up, Nova. You don't wanna talk to me right now," he warned me with those blood red eyes piercing through me. As mad as he was, his hand still found its way between my thighs.

I sucked my teeth and sat quietly for as long as I could. My body temperature started to rise, getting as heated as his. It had always been Jarvis' way since the day I met him. I'd held so much back to keep peace and grow love between us but tonight all that was about to change.

"You know what, Jarvis?" I asked, turning my body in the seat to face him. "I will not be quiet. My voice matters too. Everything has always been about you. You claim to want to make me happy but not one gah-damn mothafuckin time have you put in the effort to find out what makes me happy besides you."

I shocked myself by talking to him that way but the look on his face was priceless. He stared at me like my head was spinning. The heated energy coming from us started to fog the back windows.

"And another damn thang! I'm going to dress how I want and do what da fuck I want. You mad because I went out with friends to have some fun," I said nearly screaming at him. "You think taking me to some boring ass dinner party and fancy ass restaurant is fun. It's damn not!"

"And going to a damn club half ass dressed so niggas can insult you like trash is?" he asked angrily, causing spit to fly from his mouth. "I don't use some damn spiritual belief to sit on my ass, taking petty ass jobs to get by. I'm running a damn multi-million-dollar company."

"Humble yo damn self, nigga. Only a couple of years ago you was that nigga disrespecting females and still do," I reminded him. "Yo black ass don't complain about me being on my ass when you ask me to open my legs to fuck."

He rolled down the partition.

"Pull this shit over! I'll walk damn home!" He barked at Bahka.

"Fine!" I said, turning my body to look straight ahead.

When the car came to a stop, he jumped out never looking my way. As soon as the door closed, I let out a gut-wrenching cry. It was over. He would never forgive me for the things I said.

The partition came back down.

"Give him some time to cool off. His temper is a beast," Bahka suggested.

"I'm so sorry for getting you involved in this," I said through my sobs. "I didn't think he would get so mad."

"We get into heated arguments all the time but he's a good man. Been knowing him since he was hugging blocks," he told me. "When I got out of prison for a drug charge, he gave me a job. The nigga pay me way too much for what I do. We even argued about that."

We both laughed knowing how stubborn Jarvis was. Bahka talked about his wife and kids as he drove. I was happy for the distraction. When I got home, I took a long, hot shower, meditated and climbed in the bed with Binx beside me.

Jarvis

J got heated when I saw a picture of her on a blog dancing in that short ass dress. Seeing that made me guzzle down half a bottle of Bourbon as I made my way to the club. When it came to Nova, not only was I protective I was territorial.. Having her back in my life was a curse and a blessing. Being with her had been the happiest I'd been in a long time. The feeling of not having her in my life angered and scared me. Nova loved me but she wasn't happy with me and I didn't know how to fix that.

When I got home, I made my way to the bedroom, slowly opening the door. *I hate that damn cat!* All I could see was his eyes in the dark room. The furry bastard sat beside her on the bed eyeballing me like he was truly her protector. I didn't know if he was growling at me or purring, but the sounds reminded me of her erotic moans. Nova was lying on her stomach knocked out. The black satin sheet only covered her from the waist down; her dark skin was shining. She looked so peaceful, so I decided to leave her be.

We both needed to cool off before we talked. I had never seen Nova mad. I reminded myself never to make her that mad again. She read my black ass from front to back. My stubborn ass wouldn't even let her have her moment.

I eased the door back closed. The flight home from Cleveland had me exhausted. I crashed in the bedroom next to the master bedroom because it was the closest. The next thing I remember was trying to catch my breath from drowning in water. I wasn't dreaming about eating Nova out, so it had to be reality. I finally sat up to see Nova standing over me pouring a jug of water over my face and her other hand was on her hip.

"What da fuck, Nova?" I asked angrily, quickly standing up and snatching the jug from her hand. Nova didn't budge. She stood cemented with a furious stare on her face. I moved around her since she wouldn't move. As mad as I was, I would never attempt or make her think I would hurt her. She knew that too. That was what gave her the courage to try and drown me.

"Who da fuck is that Jarvis?" she asked, holding up and iPad.

Nona Day   Over You

"Stop damn cussing, Nova?" I said, snatching the iPad from her hand. I didn't know who she was becoming but it wasn't the Nova I fell hard for.

I looked at the screen to see a video of Nova in the club dancing. The next slide was me and a woman having a drink. I couldn't lie the picture looked shady. I threw the tablet on the bed knowing the article was a bunch of assumptions from nosey mothafuckas.

"That doesn't look like a boring conference to me," she said staring me down.

"Is you on yo damn period or something?" I asked. "If not, you need to take yo ass back to your peace space and meditate."

"Who is she, Jarvis?" she asked again. This time there wasn't anger in her voice. She was hurt and sad, so I had to explain. Hurting her was something I never wanted to do.

"She wants me to invest in her small record company. Since I was in her city, she asked me to stop by and hear a couple of her artists. I liked them enough to offer her a small investment. We went out to celebrate the deal with her artists and husband," I explained. I walked over and grabbed my phone off the nightstand and scrolled until I found what I wanted. "This the pic the blog didn't post."

It was a picture of all of us together. She took the phone and examined the picture before looking up at me with apologetic eyes.

"I'm sorry," she said shamefully.

"Get out, so I can shower," I said. It hurt to know she didn't trust me. I never thought she was at the club trying to cheat on me. My anger came from other men ogling and fantasizing about what belonged to me without me being there to protect her. I went inside the bathroom slamming the door behind me. I got the water as hot as I could stand it and turned on the jet sprays. My body started to come alive, but it felt like I was still carrying a heavy burden.

Nova pushed the sliding door open, looking scared and unsure.

"You gon' stand there or get in?" I asked. I couldn't stay mad at her for long. Even when we got into arguments, we made up in no time. The longest we'd stayed mad at each other was almost two hours. Nova had an aura about her that soothed any anger or sadness in me.

Nona Day   Over You

She got in behind me and started massaging my back. My body slowly started to relax. I kept my back to her as she got the loofa and started bathing me. I couldn't stop my dick from jumping and growing. After the suds rinsed off, she started placing kisses all over my back while reaching around to massage my dick. I turned around to face her.

"So, you gon' use sex to correct yo fuck up?" I asked with a serious face. I was over being mad when she slid the shower door open. This was just me fucking with her.

"For starters," she said, smiling and blinking the water from her long eyelashes.

She dropped to her knees and wasted no time taking my entire dick in her mouth. The inside of Nova's cheeks felt like she had suction cups. With no hands, her head bopped with my dick ramming against the back of her throat. I tried to be unimpressed, but she was working magic. Wanting to bury my dick inside her, I lift her up wrapping her legs around my waist and slammed my dick inside her. She started winding her hips as she tightened her walls around my shaft. Gripping her waist, I started bouncing her up and down my dick.

Wrapping one arm around her waist, I reached behind me and turned off the jet sprayed. I was getting ready to make her cream all over my dick and didn't want it washed away. Pinning her against the wall, I placed my right hand around her throat and started drilling inside her while tightening the grip around her neck. She looked scared at first. When she felt her orgasm building, she went wild throwing her pussy at me. The intensity of my hand around her throat and my dick spreading her walls and torturing her spots had her eyes rolling in the back of her head. Her body shook like she was seizing. With her mouth open, she started coming. Her walls had my shaft in a chokehold as she frosted my dick. I kept drilling inside her. A few minutes later, she squirted all over me.

"You gon' catch it for me?" I asked. All she could do was nod her head. I let her legs go and she dropped to the shower floor. She moaned at tasting herself on me and went to work.

"Fuck Nova! I'm bout to bust!" I groaned. She pulled my dick from her mouth and used both hands to jack it off with her mouth open to catch my cum.

"Fuuuckk! Aaaarrrggghhh!" I howled unloading in her mouth and on her face. My knees buckled when Nova swallowed my semi-hard dick. Every nerve in my body was too sensitive for what she was doing to me. I tried pulling away from her, but she wrapped her arms around my thighs, taking my dick in her mouth with no hands. I knew I sounded like a weak nigga telling her how good she was sucking me off, but I didn't give a damn. The way her mouth and tongue were making love to my dick was phenomenal. After I released my second load, all I could do was stumble backwards and flopped down on the shower bench. My breathing was erratic, so I sat there giving it time to regulate.

Nova stood up and turned the jet sprays back on. She walked over and straddled my lap.

"Ain't got shit else to give you," I told her seriously. She had drained me of everything I had.

She laughed. "I know. Am I forgiven?"

"Am I forgiven for last night?" I asked, massaging her ass cheeks.

She giggled. "You were forgiven after I said my peace."

"Man, don't cuss me no more, Nova. That shit hurt my damn feelings," I said honestly. I never wanted to cause that kind of anger from her again. She giggled.

"It was the liquor. I felt so bad after I said it all," she admitted.

"So we good?" I asked. She nodded her head and kissed my lips softly.

"It's Saturday, so I'm going to cook us some breakfast," she said, getting off my lap.

"Where you wanna go?" I asked.

"I like cooking for you on Antoine's days off. Unless you don't like my cooking," she said pouting her thick, luscious lips.

"I'm not talking about food. I mean anywhere in the world. Just me and you for five days," I said.

A big smile spread across her face with wide eyes. "For real? I nodded my head. "Can I think about it over breakfast?"

"Yea, soon as you decide we'll go," I assured her. She smothered my face with kisses, and I love yous.

Nova decided she wanted a trip to St. Barts. While Nova cooked breakfast, I planned for our flight. Thirty minutes later, we were seated at the breakfast table enjoying waffles, omelets and pork and turkey sausage with fresh fruit. She looked over and smiled.

"What?" I asked.

"I just never imagined we would be together like this," she said still smiling.

"Shit me neither," I admitted. I started thinking about when I hired Trevor to spy on her. She looked happy with her life, going to the park for yoga every day and doing numerous types of volunteer work in her small community. That was the type of person Nova was. She didn't have to know you to help you. When I saw how happy she was, I decided to let her live her life until I realized I needed her in mine.

"It hurt when I found out you was engaged," she admitted.

"Same way I felt when I saw you going on dates with niggas," I said angrily. "That's why them mothafuckas got one date and you never heard from their asses again."

Tears instantly started to fill Nova's eyes and her body trembled in fear. It took everything in me to hold my laughter in.

"Y-you killed them?" she asked horrified. I finally roared with laughter. Nova was so terrified of me at that moment that she jumped up from the table and started running upstairs. I ran after her until I tripped on her big, ugly ass, metallic, Herman Munster boot that was lying on the second flight of stairs. My ass went stumbling back down the stairs and onto the second level floor.

"Gah-damn, Nova!" I barked with anger and pain from the fall. Nova left shit everywhere in the house. She was clean but messy and disorganized as hell. I would always find shoes, clothes or something that belonged to her all over the house.

She immediately came rushing back down the stairs calling my name and kneeled down beside me. I quickly grabbed her and gently rolled on top of her.

"Jarvis, let me up! I thought you were hurt," she said angrily. She thought I killed her little boyfriends but still wanted to save me. She couldn't possibly be this perfect.

I laughed. "Nova, calm yo ass down. I ain't killed nobody. I just scared the niggas off."

"Jarvis!" she yelped angrily, trying to push me off of her. I started kissing her on the neck and her body started to relax under me.

"I didn't hurt them, Nova. Just let them know you weren't available," I said staring down at her. My hand slipped under my T-shirt that she wore and inside her panties. I started massaging her clit with my thumb while two fingers slipped inside her tight, wet pussy. "Now, that I have you, I will kill a nigga about you, Nova."

She wanted to respond but the way my fingers were working her pussy had her speechless. She arched her back and started winding her hips, fucking my fingers until she exploded on my hand.

Two hours later, we were packing to go to St. Barts for five days. It took her forever to choose an animal daycare for Binx. That damn cat still hated my ass, and I still stayed away from him. One night Nova and I were arguing, and his black ass hissed at me in an attack mode. I hauled ass outta the bedroom.

Nova was ecstatic talking about all the things she wanted to do. When my phone rang, I stepped out of the bedroom and quickly answered.

"Mr. Alexandria, this is Mr. Singleton's assistant, Mrs. Chancy. I'm calling on his behalf to invite you to his home for a meeting in two days," she said.

This was one of the biggest business endeavors of my career. Mr. Singleton was successful and the most knowledgeable candidate to make this project happen. Turning down his invitation to discuss this project could cost me the opportunity to have the best on my board. Nova was going to be pissed but we could visit St. Barts or anywhere else another time. I had to accept this invite.

"Yes, Mrs. Chancy. I'm more than happy to accept his invite," I said.

"That's great. I'll be sending you an itinerary to your company email," Mrs. Chancy informed me. "Oh, and Mr. Singleton wanted me to inform you that you are more than welcome to bring your lady friend."

"Thank you so much," I said.

After the call ended, I took a deep breath. There was nothing I could say or do to make this go over easy, so I walked back into the bedroom to crush her heart. When I walked back into the room, she immediately knew something was wrong.

"What's wrong?" she asked worriedly.

"Nova, we can't go on this trip. A big opportunity just came up and I gotta take it," I said, seeing the joy fade away from her face. "I'm leaving for Miami in the morning. I know it's not St. Barts, but I want you to come with me."

"Thanks but I'll just stay here. I need to work in the greenhouse and canning room anyway. I'm going to start peddling some of my oils and herbal blends," she said with a deflated voice.

"Nova, I'm sorry," I said, walking over to her.

"It's okay, Jarvis. I understand," she said never looking at me. "I'll help you pack."

She didn't say much as she helped me pack. After we were done, she put on some clothes and went to her greenhouse. I went to my man cave, rolled a blunt and grabbed a bottle. It made me feel like shit to disappoint her. After drowning myself in my own misery, I fell asleep. When I woke up the sun was down, and Nova was nowhere in the house. The thought that she had left me caused me to panic; I found my phone. Before I could call her, I saw she had sent me a text.

Went to my parents

Be back later

I instantly got a sick feeling in the pit of my stomach. What Nova said made sense. She was happy with me, but not with the life I had to offer her. My life consisted of business deals, networking with snobs and traveling. After taking a shower, I slipped on some boxers. For some reason my eyes zoomed in on Nova's meditation/prayer section in the living area by the window. She had chosen the perfect spot. I remember watching her once when the brightness of the sunrise was coming through the window shining light on her beauty.

Not being much of a prayer, I decided to give it a try. I needed help from God to do this shit right with her. He needed to step da fuck up and show me how to make her happy in my life. I lit a couple of the candles and kneeled down on one of the pillows to start my prayer.

Nova

*H*eartbroken wasn't a strong enough word to describe how disappointed I was about not going on our trip. I hadn't truly enjoyed mother nature since I'd been back with Jarvis. Sometimes I felt trapped in his world. I never complained because I loved him so much. Being with him consisted of adapting to his lifestyle which was totally different from mine. Jarvis' life was dedicated to making deals, work and more work. He never really took the time to enjoy the fruits of his labor. A simple walk in the park was too much for him because his life was so busy.

I loved traveling and seeing all the beauty the world had to offer. It was necessary to my well-being to take time to enjoy the beauty of this world. Being confined to a job only to make millions of dollars that you couldn't enjoy wasn't living. I'd never worked with the goal of securing wealth. I worked for the simple necessities in life and the rest of my money was spent on what made me happy.

Nona Day   Over You

I spent hours in the greenhouse and canning room. After I was done, I cooked dinner for us. I went to find Jarvis; he was knocked out in his man cave smelling like a liquor still. I decided to let him sleep it off, so I went to visit my parents.

When I got back home, I noticed Jarvis was awake. He never texted me back, so I knew he was still upset that I wouldn't go on the business trip to Miami with him. I made my way to the bedroom and was blown away by seeing Jarvis on his knees in my prayer section. Jarvis never joined me for meditation or prayer. It was wrong of me to eavesdrop, but I couldn't walk away.

"Okay second highest to the top OG. They say I'm supposed to talk to you about my problems. I guess you the middleman between me and the top dog. I'm not exactly sure how I'm supposed to do this shit, but here it goes." He began his prayer talking to Jesus. I wasn't religious but I understood that all Christian prayers are spoken to Jesus. I had to cover my mouth to hold in the giggle inside me. I stood and continued to listen.

"I'm fucking up big time with her. Trying to balance this love shit and my life is some stressful ass shit. I ain't trying to give up neither one, so I need you to help a nigga out. Ain't no way you brought her back in my life only for her to leave me again. You can't be that gah-damn cruel. I know I've done some fucked up shit, but I'm trying to do right for her. Just work with me and help me out on this time. In Jesus name, I pray," he said ending his prayer. "Oh and thanks for giving me another chance with her."

I quickly left the room before he spotted me. Tears fell from my eyes at the thought of him truly trying his best to love me. Here I was only thinking of myself. I silently crept back down to the first flight of stairs and started calling his name as if I had just arrived back home. I walked in the bedroom and he was sitting on side of the bed.

"You finally woke up," I said, smiling and walking over to him, sitting down beside him.

"Yea," he answered dryly. Like a second instinct, his hand went between my thighs. At first, I thought he always wanted sex when he did it. But now I realized it was a way for him to absorb my energy. I didn't even think he realized why he did it.

"I cooked. Did you eat?" I asked.

"Nah, didn't have much of an appetite when I woke up," he said. He looked down at me. "I thought you fuckin' left me again, Nova," he said with anguish in his voice.

I took the hand that was between my thighs and laced his fingers with mine and smiled at him.

"It's going to take more than a raincheck on St. Barts to run me away," I replied. I straddled his lap. "Is the invite to Miami still open?"

Happiness filled his eyes. He rolled me onto the bed on my back.

"I promise the trip won't be all business," he assured me.

"Oh don't worry, I'm going to make sure of that," I said.

He smiled down at me.

"We taking the elevator downstairs," he said smiling.

We made our way to the elevator. Jarvis kept sending the elevator up and down as we sexed each other like crazy. After we were done, we ate dinner. Since Jarvis was already packed, I went upstairs to pack my things.

Miami, Florida

Jarvis didn't get us some fancy hotel suite. He got me the most amazing beach house. The view was breathtaking. We were so close to the beautiful beach I could smell the seawater and hear the waves. It was a one level house painted in red, orange bright yellow and green,. The house felt so lively and welcoming. My mouth dropped open when I walked into the bedroom. An enormous round bed was in the air hanging from the ceiling. Rainbow colored drapes were all around the bed. The walls in the bedroom were painted bright orange. Colorful themes weren't Jarvis' style, but I loved the vibrant colors. I knew he chose this house for me.

"How we supposed to get on the bed?" I asked Jarvis. He walked over and grabbed a remote from the nightstand. He stood behind me wrapping his arm around my waist. Placing soft wet kisses on my neck, he used the remote to descend the bed. The iron ropes attached from the ceiling to the bed slowly lowered the bed to the floor.

"I can't wait to fuck the shit outta you in midair," he whispered, nibbling on my ear. I giggled as my walls throbbed at the thought of it. I turned around to face him with a big smile on my face.

Nona Day   Over You

"I'm so glad I came. I'm sorry for not being more receptive to your life," I said.

He kissed me softly on my lips. "As long as you keep being receptive to this dick, we good."

I laughed and shook my head. We wanted a quickie on the bed but based on the itinerary we were scheduled to be at Jarvis' business associate's house for dinner in an hour. By the time we got dressed, a limo was waiting outside for us.

To make sure I represented Jarvis well, I wore one of the outfits Sandy had bought me. It was a black, high waist, calf length, skirt that contoured to my frame with a poplin two-bow waist blouse that I loved. Including the Versace signature ankle straps on my feet and the bra I wore, my entire outfit was over five thousand dollars. Just the thought of how much money I was wearing was outlandish, but damn I looked good.

Not having time to do anything with my hair, I had to go with my natural, kinky, wild state. I pinned it back from my face with a couple of designed hair pins. Like usual, Jarvis didn't seem impressed with my clean up. He truly didn't care what I wore. In his eyes, I was just as beautiful in my ugly clothes, as he called them.

Nona Day   Over You

When we got in the back of the limo, Jarvis realized the skirt stopped his hand from having access to its resting place between my thighs. He needed to feel that I was good with this, so I laced my fingers between his. He closed his eyes and laid his head back until we arrived at our destination. The limo driver punched the code in at the security gate and drove up the long curved driveway.

The front door to the extravagant Miami mansion opened just as we reached the front door. A young, beautiful Puerto Rican woman opened the door dressed as eloquent and stylish as me. She welcomed us inside, and Jarvis introduced me to her. I tried not to seem awestruck but the look on my face showed that I wasn't used to seeing such an enormous home. It wasn't the décor of the home; it was the size. I thought Jarvis' mansion was huge, but this one was gigantic.

"Oh my God, I love that blouse," she said examining my outfit.

"Thank you; I love your entire outfit and your beautiful home," I said graciously. She seemed like a nice girl. I knew she couldn't have been no more than twenty-five years old.

"Thank you so much. Cornell is in his smoke room. Patrice will escort you while I give Nova a tour," she said.

As we toured her home, we made small talk about ourselves. Abril wasn't like any of the uppity people I was used to meeting while out with Jarvis. She was down to earth and funny. Like me, she didn't have a career. Her career consisted of satisfying her husband which she didn't seem to have a problem with. The young lady I spent time with touring the home was different than the one sitting at the dinner table. She was relaxed, funny and energetic earlier. Now, she sat still as a rock, quiet and sophistication oozed from her. It made me wonder how much she had to change to fit in Cornell's life.

"How long have you been with Mr. Alexandria?" Abril asked me.

"Only a few months, but we've been friends for a while," I said.

"I can tell you're not quite comfortable in your role with him," she said smiling. "Trust me, you'll get used to it."

"How much did you have to change to get comfortable in Mr. Cornell's life?" I asked.

Nona Day   Over You

She laughed. "Girl, I was a wild child, partying every damn night until I met him at a night club. My life slowly changed. Now I attend brunch, tea parties and all the other fancy events with the rich and powerful."

"Do you like it?" I asked.

She shrugged her shoulders. "I miss being the old me sometimes, but it's the price I had to pay to live this lifestyle.

I followed Abril to what was called the smoke room. Jarvis and Cornell sat on each end of a sofa sipping some type of brown cognac and smoking a cigar.

"Gentlemen, dinner is served," Abril announced. Jarvis introduced me to Cornell. I'm not going to say she was with Cornell for his money, but she definitely had herself a sugar daddy. Cornell looked to be in his late fifties and very handsome. He had chocolate skin with salt and pepper hair, beard and mustache. It was obvious he worked out because his body was toned like he was young man

They stood up and we followed the couple to the dining room with Jarvis' hand in the small of my back. His entire demeanor was different. These are the moments of

Jarvis I rarely saw. And the Jarvis I knew; the outside world never saw.

We had small talk over a four-course meal. I enjoyed talking to Cornell. Like me, he enjoyed nature and loved traveling to exotic places.

Every time Jar spoke, I had to look at him. No matter how many times I saw this poised, refined gentleman I was amazed. He talked with Cornell about things I had no idea he had knowledge of. The collegiate words that came from him, his political knowledge, his ideology of the inequality of blacks and minorities and women's right left me wanting to slide under the table and suck the life out of him. Seeing Jarvis this way made me wonder would being in his life completely change me. I wondered who I become so consumed with living lavishly that I forget who I am.

I looked over at Abril who seemed bored with the conversation between Jarvis and Cornell, so I tried making small talk with her. She had no hobbies and it seemed as if her world revolved around Cornell. I didn't want to be an arm piece for Jarvis. It made me look at myself in Jarvis' life in a different light. Supporting Jarvis wasn't a problem for me, but I didn't want that to be all I was in my life. Changing who I am to fit into his corporate life to mingle with his colleagues could cause me to lose myself. Cornell was one of the few that I could dine with every night. He wasn't like the other colleagues that threw shade that they thought went over our heads. It was painful to sit quietly and not go off in fear of damaging Jarvis' reputation with his associates. Jarvis was relaxed and enjoying the time with Cornell unlike other dinner parties. It warmed my heart to see him finally enjoying a business dinner.

"I've extended an invitation for Jarvis to play golf with me tomorrow, but he informed me he doesn't play," Cornell said.

"I play," I blurted out. I loved playing any sport that was outside. "I'm not PGA material, but I'm pretty good."

"You do?" Jarvis asked surprised.

"Yea; just haven't played in a couple of years. I had a college friend that invited me to his family's country club often," I informed them.

"Well, our mates can chauffer us around on the carts while we play," Cornell suggested.

For the first time, I had met acquaintances of Jarvis' that I actually wanted to spend time with. After dinner, I made sure to give my compliments to the chef for the succulent Cornish hen and sweet carrots.

We ended up going out with them that night to a club where Cornell had a VIP sky box. The club was a mixture of all races. After drinking enough wine to loosen us up, Abril and I made our way to the dance floor. I was having the time of my life with all the flashing lights and fast upbeat music. It would make anyone tap their feet.

By the time we made it back to the beach house, the sun was starting to rise. I still wasn't sleepy, so I sat on the deck watching the sun rise. Jarvis walked out on the deck with no clothes on and a rock-hard rod. He relaxed in the lounger next to me.

"Get out them damn clothes and come ride this dick," he said, holding his dick. He didn't have to tell me twice. My Jarvis had returned so I peeled my clothes off as quickly as I could. Instead of straddling him face to face, I faced the rising sun, sliding down on him.

"Fuck Nova," he groaned. Slow and steady I started winding my hips. I could feel his shaft pulsating and spreading against my walls. My hands massaged my breasts and fingers pinched and plucked my hard nipples. Jarvis sat up spreading his legs on each side of the lounger causing my legs to open wider. His crown poked at my overly sensitive spot causing my juices to flood his lap. He wrapped one arm around my waist and the other started stroking my swollen bud. His tongue licked and sucked all over my back and shoulders while his teeth dug softly into my skin.

"Keep fucking me, Nova. This pussy so mothafuckin' good," he groaned. I turned into an undefeated champion bull rider on him. Swaying, grinding, winding and bucking on him while I came uncontrollably.

The sun was up and shining down on us as I was showering him with my essence.

"Gaaahhh dammmmnn! Fuuuccck!" Jarvis barked before sinking his teeth into my shoulder to muffle the grizzly roar coming from the pit of his stomach. His rod jumped while unloading inside of me.

We stayed in the position until we came down from our sexually induced high. When the feeling in my legs returned, I finally stood up.

"Damn," Jarvis said looking down at his cream covered pelvis area. My juices had soaked into the bottom half of the cushion.

We made our way in the house and showered together. Experiencing the bed in mid-air would have to be saved for another night. We were spending the day golfing with the Singletons and the night on Cornell's yacht.

I curled up in the bed with Jarvis for a few hours of sleep before it was time to wake up.

Jarvis

After watching Nova and Cornell play golf, we had a few drinks at his country club. I was having a good time, but to see Nova enjoying life the way she wanted was priceless. After leaving the country club, Nova and Abril went sightseeing. Cornell and I went back to his home to discuss a few projects we thought of investing in together.

When the ladies returned, we made our way to the yacht. Even though it was January, the weather was perfect. Nova had on a two-piece bathing suit that showed of her slender curves. I had to pat myself on the back, because that ass was getting fat. She always complained about the size of her breasts, but they were perfect to me. My mouth couldn't stay away from them and I loved making her squirm when I lapped my tongue around the dark circles on her breasts.

The yacht took us to a restaurant where we had dinner. When we returned back to the yacht, we all sat on the deck. After a couple of hours, the Singletons turned in for the night. Nova wanted to enjoy the moonlight and night breeze. I grabbed a throw blanket from our cabin for her. She laid between my legs with her back against my chest as the yacht took us back to the shore.

"Jarvis, what kind of business deal are you making with Cornell?" she asked. Nova never asked about my business. I always assumed it was a part of my life she cared nothing about.

"I'm trying to get enough investors to open a black owned bank. He would be the perfect candidate for the chairman. All of this is to see if I'm worthy of having him," I said.

She sat and turned to face me with her eyes looking as if they were going to pop out her head. I couldn't help but laugh.

"A bank?" she asked. "I thought maybe you were looking to invest in some kind of resort or something. A bank if effing huge, Jarvis."

"I know. That's why I've been taking so many damn trips. Everything I'm doing is to make it happen," I told her.

"Is he going to do it?" she asked.

"I don't know yet. I need to get a lot of shit lined up before he decides. He needs to know who's all investing in the bank. I'm still seeking out investors," I told her.

"Jarvis Michael Alexandria, I'm so proud of you," she said sincerely.

"Thanks, Nova Lee Champagne," I said smiling. She giggled. "When all this is over, we'll be able to do shit like this more often."

"Seeing you the last few days has been crazy. You're like a chameleon. I see the rude, abrasive, hood guy but they see a dignified, charismatic gentlemen," she said.

"It's hell trying to balance the two, Nova," I said seriously. "But people like Cornell would never give time to the old Jarvis."

"Which Jarvis do you prefer being?" she asked.

"The one that gets your love," I admitted.

"They both share the same heart, so I love them both equally," she said smiling at me.

My life was so twisted into who I was and who I am. The only time I got to be the real me was when I was with Nova. There was no judging or disappointment in her eyes when she looked at me. Being the charismatic gentlemen was a necessity to give everyone else what they wanted from me. As I spent more time with Nova, I wanted to just live my life as myself, but no one else wanted that me in their lives.

"And you get the same dick," I said jokingly. She laughed. Things were quiet for a few minutes.

"Jarvis, Amoy said you went through a lot after I left. What happened?" she asked. That was some shit I didn't care to discuss, because it brought back the anger and sadness I had inside of me.

"Nova, let that shit go. Amoy talks too damn much. Life is good now," I said. She felt the irritation in my voice because she left me sitting out on the deck in my thoughts.

I hated to think about how fucked up I was after Aunt Belle's death. Spending time with Nova was the only thing that kept me sane. After she left, I didn't give a damn about how my life was. I was in a fog as I wreaked havoc silently. I was so messed up in the head and heart I didn't even realize I was building an empire around me until I had it in the palm of my hands. With so much power, I thought I would be happy accomplishing my father's goals for him, but I wasn't.

SOUL Publications

Nona Day   Over You

A long talk with my father's old connect revealed my father's true goals. I still had work to do. My father was the charismatic gentlemen, so I became him to make the moves needed to position myself in the place I am now, a young black man on the verge of opening an all African American bank with all black board members.

I pulled myself from my thoughts and went inside the cabin. I stripped down to my boxers and got in the bed beside Nova. She wasn't asleep, because I could feel her tense up when I pulled her toward me.

"You better not be pouting about dumb shit, Nova," I said.

She sat up and turned around to face me. "Don't tell me how I should feel, Jarvis. Outside of sex you never share yourself with me. I want to connect with you more than just sexually."

"What da fuck else is there?" I asked.

"Emotionally, mentally and spiritually. I know there's pain inside of you that you don't share," she said. "The drunken nights after trips and events. What's all that about?"

Nona Day   Over You

"I just be missing yo pigeon toed ass," I said half telling the truth. She giggled, gently pushing my shoulder. She rested her head on my shoulder. "When you left, it was just me. There was no one to keep me calm. I took on the most ruthless drug empires head on, not caring if I lived or died. Killing niggas that even attempted to cross me. I was living life like a ticking time bomb, doing reckless shit without considering the consequences.

"I'm going to be more supportive, and take trips with you," she said.

It was hard being away from her when I had to take trips. The other truth was it was so hard trying to be someone I wasn't, sucking up to rich privileged folks that I knew looked down on me. I was starting to hate that person. But that person was necessary to accomplish my goals and had become a part of me. I didn't need Nova in my head trying to analyze me. All I needed her to do was be there for me, to be the person that loved me regardless.

"Now, tell me about you selling your products," I said. I listened intently and she seemed excited about it. I offered to invest but she wasn't ready to put that much work into it. If she wasn't ready, I wasn't going to force her, but I let her know the offer would always stand.

A Couple of Days Later

We said our goodbyes to Cornell and Abril. He told me once I had gotten enough investors to reach out to him. If he approved of everyone, he was on board. I knew plenty of people with the money to invest but image mattered, so that canceled most of them out. The others were caught up in scandals or criminal activity that was known worldwide. I still ran a drug empire, but I ran my shit like a corporation, and no one could connect any illegal activity back to me.

Nova and I decided to stay an extra two days just to enjoy some time to ourselves. Tonight, we were at a club Nova wanted to attend. I sat back and chilled while she enjoyed herself on the dance floor. I actually liked the outfit she was wearing tonight. She wore a pair of black and white sprite ruffled wide leg pants and a dark red long sleeved, over the shoulder, crop top. I had the perfect view of her, and she was putting on a show just for me. Her dark chocolate skin glistened under flashing colorful lights.. There were a couple of men that couldn't take their eyes off her, but I knew she was going home with me.

After Nova was done dancing, she came over and sat next to me. My hand instantly went between her thighs. She looked at me biting down on her bottom lip. It was time to go. Nova had no idea how sexy she was.

"Let's go," I said.

"Let me use the restroom before we go," she said, standing up.

I stayed seated to wait for her. Ten minutes later, she returned to the table with two young ladies. One was Caucasian, the other was an African American.

"I met them in the bathroom. They're from Atlanta. They just got married and are on their honeymoon," Nova informed me.

"Hi, nice to meet you. You're very handsome," the white girl said. She didn't try to hide the fact that she wanted to fuck me.

"Thank you and congratulations. Many blessings," I said, shaking both their hands.

"You're very lucky. Nova is absolutely stunning," the black girl said looking at Nova.

"Yes she is," I agreed looking at Nova with a smile.

"We aren't going to interrupt your vacation any longer. Here's our phone number if you decide to take us up on our offer," the Caucasian girl said. She handed Nova a piece of paper with her eyes on me.

I looked at Nova with a puzzled look. The girls stood up, said their goodbyes and walked away holding hands. Nova looked at me with a smile.

"What offer?" I asked without a smile.

"They wanted us to have a foursome with them. The white girl likes you. The black one gotta thing for me," she said searching my face for confirmation.

"Come on, it's time to take your ass back to the room," I said angrily, standing up.

"What you getting mad for?" she asked still seated. "I know you like women with big butts and breasts."

"Shut da fuck up and come on!" I barked.

The ride back to the beach house was completely silent. I couldn't believe she would let me fuck another woman or have the audacity to think I would be cool with another woman touching her. Maybe Nova was starting to feel trapped being with just me. She was used to living free.

Being in a relationship restricted her from doing certain things, but I never thought she was that freaky.

When we arrived back at the house, I went straight to the bathroom and stripped out of my clothes. Nova was sitting on the bed naked., She looked at me when I walked out.

"Why are you mad?" she asked, walking over to me. "Men like that kind of stuff. I've heard you mention threesomes you've had with several women."

"Those damn women wasn't you, Nova. And you ain't them so stop trying to do dumb shit that ain't in you," I said.

"I'm not trying to be them," she said. "Abril said men like you and Cornell need variety. I'm just—"

I cut her off before she could finish her sentence.

"Shut da—" I said before Nova cut me off with a hard ass slap across my face.

The sting of her slap burned my face but the shock of her actually doing it had me stuck. If she had been anyone else, she would've felt my wrath, but this was Nova. *My fuckin' heart.* Before my brain could tell me to react, Nova dashed inside the bathroom locking the door behind her. I walked over and banged on the door.

"Nova, open the damn door!" I demanded.

"No! Stop talking to me like I'm a damn child!" she screamed on the other side of the door. I decided to calm my voice.

"Nova, I'm sorry. Just open the door," I said. "Please."

After a few seconds, she unlocked and slowly opened the door. She looked up, batting her long lashes at me. I could tell she had been crying.

"I'm sorry for hitting you," she said softly, dropping her head. I lifted her head by her chin.

"Did you think I was going to hit you?" I asked. She shrugged her shoulders. "Nova, I would take my own life before I lay a hand on you to hurt you."

She wrapped her arms around my waist, laying her head on my chest.

"I'm sorry for trying to bring others in on what we have together," she said.

"Come on. Let's talk," I said, tapping her on the ass and lifting her up. She wrapped her legs around my waist, and I carried her to the bed. "Now, tell me what Abril said before I rudely interrupted you."

"It's not important," she said.

"Yea the fuck it is if she got you trying to get yo pussy ate by a bitch and have me fucking her wife," I reminded her. She laughed and covered her face shamefully. "Yea, see how dumb that shit sound."

"I just don't want you to get bored with having sex with me. She said she keeps things interesting with Cornell by bringing other women in," she explained.

"Why do you fuck me, Nova?" I asked. "I mean besides this dick is lethal."

She laughed. "I have sex with you to express my love, to feel your energy, to connect with you and because you make me cum, I mean you *really* make me cum."

I laughed. "We ain't Cornell and Abril. What they got, ain't what we got. Maybe they need extra people in their bedroom or maybe that's their way of expressing love. We don't need that. At least I don't."

"I don't either, Jarvis," she said quickly.

Nona Day   Over You

I reached behind me and grabbed the remote. She wrapped her arms around my neck as the bed ascended in the air. My legs were hanging off the bed. Nova finally let me go and looked around. She lifted up and slowly slid down on my dick.

"Hold on to the drapes," I told her. "I ain't gon' let you fall."

She leaned forward and slid her tongue in my mouth. With our tongues deep inside each other's mouths, she grabbed the drapes. Her arms were extended like she was nailed to a cross. Breaking our kiss, I gave her breasts all my attention. The more I made love to her breasts the more she made love to my dick. I started massaging her clit. Her head fell back as she moaned in ecstasy. She looked so damn hot riding my dick. We fucked until I wanted to taste her juices that had drenched my dick. I lifted her up throwing her legs over my shoulders.

"Jarvis," she moaned still holding onto the drapes.

"I got you," I reminded her with her glistening pussy in my face. I feasted on her until I sucked the strength from her body. Her juices saturated my face and spilled down my chest and stomach. I didn't want to stop tasting her, but she was too weak to hold on. I grabbed her around the waist and fell backwards. Nova yelped thinking she was falling but landed with her hands on the bed, positioned on all fours. She rode my face until I slid her down on my dick. The sun came up before we stopped fucking. I lowered the bed when she fell asleep with her head on my chest.

These last few days had been perfect. Tomorrow it was time to return back to reality. I had to try and find a balance between my world with her and the outside world.

A Week Later

Nova

$\mathcal{I}$ sat in the middle of the bed waiting patiently for Jarvis to come home from one his dinner functions. Binx sat beside me with his eyes glued to the door waiting for Jarvis to enter. They had a strange love hate relationship that I thought was cute. When my eyes got tired of waiting, I sent Binx out of the room. After saying a quick prayer, I easily and quickly doze off to sleep. I was awakened by Jarvis' voice and loud rumbling as if someone was falling. I quickly sat up in the bed and turn on the lights by the remote control. Jarvis came staggering from my prayer area. I quickly climbed out of the bed to make sure he was okay. He reeked of alcohol and weed. I didn't mind the weed aroma, but I hated the smell of alcohol oozing from his pores.

"Jarvis, you're drunk," I said walking up to him. I looked over at my small prayer area to see it was destroyed. Candles, incense, and crystals were scattered everywhere.

"I know," he said laughing.

"Come on, you need to take a shower," I said. "Your breath stinks."

"You taking one with me?" He asked staggering toward the bathroom.

"Yea, I'll take one with you," I said walking inside the bathroom with him. He leaned against the bathroom counter and started stripping out his suit. Jarvis was a neat freak but tonight he didn't care where he put his clothes. They were sprawled all over the bathroom floor. I turned on the shower using the jet sprays while he unloaded his bladder. Stepping in the shower, I waited for him to join me. He came inside and sat down on the shower bench leaning his head back with his eyes closed. I walked over and straddled his lap as the jet sprays cascaded our bodies. He lifted his head and stared at me with his drunken eyes.

"Had too much fun tonight?" I asked smiling at him.

"Ain't shit fun about dealing with mothafuckas I don't like and pretending to be some shit I ain't to get what I need," he said.

"Then why do you do it?" I asked. "You should never be something you're not to satisfy anyone."

He cocked his head to the side with his eyes glued to me.

"Is that easy huh?" He asked. I felt sarcasm in his question.

"Yes, it is," I replied. "I'm never going to be something I'm not to get anyone's approval. They accept me for who I am or not. It doesn't matter to me."

He chuckled. "That's easy for you to say since you ain't trying to have shit."

His words were laced with cruelty. I slowly stood from his lap. Just because I didn't want a career only to have money didn't mean I didn't want anything. Jarvis would never understand that because he never cared to know what I wanted. Even during our friendship, he showed no interest in knowing what I was passionate about or what I didn't like.

I wrapped a towel around me and sat on side of the bed lighting a blunt. After a few hits, my body started relaxing. Jarvis walked out of the bathroom and stared at me.

"You ain't here to give me advice about my business life," he said. "If I want your opinion, I'll ask."

Nona Day   Over You

Never had he been this mean to me. Even when he was being disrespectful, I never took it personal because I knew it wasn't done maliciously. This time was different. He was intentionally trying to use me to vent his frustration. Being here to for any other reason I can deal with, but I won't be his punching bag with cruel and hurtful comments.

"Well, why am I here Jarvis?" I asked. "All we do is have sex and you leave me here all day with nothing to do."

"I take you to parties all the damn time,"," he stated angrily.

After the several exhausting events and they were all the same. My tongue was bruised from biting it to keep from cussing everyone out. I had to remind myself I was there with Jarvis and didn't want to embarrass him. At the same time I hated I was shrinking who I was by listening to the privilege talk as if I and my people were beneath them.

"You don't even like going to those events," I said, standing up snapping back at him in the same tone. "So, what makes you think I want to keep going to them. There's nothing fun about listening to entitled people talk to us as if we should be grateful to be in their presence."

He stepped in my space.

"Because I fuckin' asked you to. I'm doing what I have to do to build a life for us."

"This isn't about us. Everything is about you," I said raising my voice. This was so not me. I've always prided myself in remaining calm and level-headed, but Jarvis was getting me completely out of character. The sad part was I was willing to put up with this behavior to be near him.

He placed his hand on my chin lifting it so I can look him in the eyes.

"Everything *was* about me getting over you," he said. "Let's not forget that. The way this shit going you making it really easy."

I couldn't stop the tears from forming in my eyes. To hear those words with some much bitterness weakened me. Somewhere in my heart, I wanted this to be about us. But this was all about him.

He walked away from me and over to the dresser. I turned around to watch him slip on a pair of boxers and tee shirt. Without saying another word to me, he walked out of the bedroom. I climbed back into the bed and let a view tears fall before falling to sleep.

Next Morning

I was awakened by Binx jumping into the bed with me. A few seconds later, a still angry Jarvis barged into the bedroom.

"Keep that damn cat out of my man cave," he said staring at Binx. "Mothafucka looking at my fish tanks like he wanna jump in there."

"He doesn't want your fish Jarvis," I said rolling my eyes at him.

"Just keep him out of there," he stated again. He looked around the bedroom. "And just because I have housekeepers don't mean you can't attempt to keep shit organized in here."

"Not my fault you came in drunk knocking things over," I said climbing out of bed. "And the mess on the floor is your clothes."

He didn't reply as he walked into the bathroom. I made my way over to my prayer area, straighten everything and picked up his clothes he had pulled from his dresser last night. Jarvis came out of the bathroom with a towel wrapped around him and walked into the closet. I followed him inside, standing behind him and wrapping my arms around his waist.

"Whatever you're going through. I'm here for you,," I said planting soft kissing on his back. "I know what a remarkable man you are. I just want you to know that also."

He turned around to face me. Jarvis didn't know how to feel about himself, so I felt it necessary to remind him how amazing he was. I should've been furious with him for how he talked to me last night, but I needed to be his serenity. Being his peace was draining but necessary to make our relationship work.

"How you do that shit Nova?" He asked turning to face me. "I just treated you like shit and you here complimenting me."

I smiled up at him. "Because I know you're only venting. I don't take it personally, but I hate you're dealing with so much that stresses and frustrates you."

"I can handle it," he said. "I'm going down to get something to eat. You coming?"

"In a few," I said. "I'm going to do some yoga in the backyard first."

Nona Day   Over You

After slipping on a pair of yoga shorts and tank top, I left out of the room and went to the backyard to do yoga. For thirty minutes, I cleared my mind and absorbed the peaceful sound of nature. Jarvis had a remarkable home, but the land was heaven with green grass and trees.

Jarvis was sitting down at the breakfast table eating when I walked inside. I prepared a plate of fruit and walked out of the breakfast room, sitting at the kitchen table to eat. He came out of the breakfast room and sat across from me. I could feel his eyes glaring at me even though my head was down.

"You wanna go to an art show and auction with me today?" He asked. I loved beautiful painting an artwork, so it warmed my heart we would do something I enjoyed. I looked up and smiled at him.

"I would love to go," I said. His face showed perplexity. "Are you sure you want me to go with you?"

"I'm positive," he said. "This event is formal with some snobbish people just so you're aware."

"I can handle it," I tried convincing myself. "This is something I can enjoy regardless."

"Okay, it starts at seven," he said. There was a quiet pause between us. "Sorry about all the fucked up shit I said last night."

"Do you want me to leave?" I asked sadly. "I know it's hasn't been easy having me back in your life. So much has changed with you and I don't seem to fit in anywhere anymore. I seem to be adding more to your plate than you can barely handle."

He gazed at me for a few minutes. "You fit in perfectly. I don't know what to do with you Nova, but I'm not letting you leave me again."

My entire body relaxed, because I didn't want to leave him.

"Okay, I guess I better spend the day getting dolled up," I said smiling. "I'm going to get a mani and pedi, get my hair done and choose one of those beautiful dresses upstairs to wear. I'm going to look like a black princess."

He laughed. "You already that Nova Lee Champagne."

"Jarvis I know I'm not here to advise you how to handle your business," I said. "I just want you to know I'm here to talk to anytime you want. I'm a great listener without being judgmental."

"It's enough you have to deal with me. You're not here to give me advice…just peace," he said. "I know I'm not easy to deal with…never have been. You always stuck with me though. I appreciate that shit."

"I'll make sure to represent you well at the auction," I said smiling. It was my mission to try harder to make him happy with my presence in his life. If attending events was what I had to do, then I'll keep doing it..

Later That Evening

I stood in front of the dresser placing the diamond stud earrings Jarvis had bought me in my ears. I truly looked like a black princess with my hair pinned up in a neat bun with small sparkling diamond hairpins,. My over the shoulder black gown with a long split fitted perfectly. My red bottoms open toed shoes showed off my incognito colored painted toenails that matched my fingernails. With just a touch of makeup I was ready to go.

Jarvis walked up behind be looking debonair in his black and white tux, wrapping his arms around my waist. His soft wet kisses on my neck sent shivers down my spine and throbbing sensations between my thighs. I knew I was risking my heart with him, but the feelings he gave me were worth it. My body reacted to his every touch, the look of desire in his eyes, and the agonizing hunger in his voice for me.

"You ready?" He asked nibbling on my earlobe and sliding his hand between my thighs. I wanted to forget the auction and have him do as he may with me, but this was an event I wanted to attend.

"Not if you keep doing that?" I told him, still unsure if I wanted him to stop. He didn't seem to be too interested in attending the event as he slipping his hand farther up my thigh. It was downright shameful how much I craved him. Just as his hand slid into my thong, his phone rang. He finally released me and answered his phone.

"A'ight, we headed down," he said before ending the call. "Bahka's waiting."

I smiled at him and held his hand as he led me out of the bedroom. When we made outside, Bahka was standing by the limo waiting for us. Jarvis walked to the opposite to let his self in.

"Y'all looking like Barack and Michelle tonight," Bahka said jokingly.

"Nigga, get in damn car and drive," Jarvis said. "Always wanna damn joke and shit.

Bahka just laughed as he made his way to the driver's seat. As soon as the limo pulled off, Jarvis hand rested between my thighs.

"I'm going to get a job and put my degree to use," I said.

"Don't be doing that because of the fucked up shit I said last night," he said. "I know you wanna do something you're passionate about. Just find out what that is."

"I just don't want you to think I'm lazy and useless," I confessed.

"I know you're not lazy Nova," he said. "But I don't want you wasting your life doing nothing because you're too smart and talented for that."

"I'll take some time and think about what I really want to do," I said. He squeezed my thigh gently acknowledging he was satisfied with my answer for now. We made small talk about the auction we were attending.

*****

Nona Day   Over You

When we arrived at the auction, Jarvis escorted me inside with my hand in his. I scan the room looking at the eloquent dresses and stylish tuxedos everyone was wearing. There had to be a crowd of over fifty people, but I could count the number of blacks on one hand, me and Jarvis included. I gladly took a glass of champagne when the waiter came around with a tray. A couple of men approached Jarvis as we made our way through the room. He introduced me, but neither showed interest in knowing me. That was fine with me. My reason for coming was to see beautiful artwork. They started talking business, so I quietly slipped away. I didn't know much about art, but I knew beauty when I saw it. The sculptures were define. As I stood admiring an exquisite sculpture, a white, middle aged woman that looked like she needed to eat a couple of more meals approached me.

"This is a beautiful piece," she said staring at the sculpture. She turned to give me her attention. "Hi, I'm Heather. I saw you enter with Jarvis. He's business partners with my husband, Paul."

"Hi Heather, it's nice to me you. I'm Nova," I said nicely. "Yes, the sculpture is stunning."

"What do you do?" She asked. My instant reaction was to go off, but I remembered Jarvis. It always seemed as if wealthy people wanted to compare their financial statuses to their peers. My monetary value has absolutely nothing to do with who I am as a person.

"I just move back to Atlanta, so I'm in between jobs," I said nicely.

"Oh don't worry, I'm sure you'll find something," she said. "In the meantime you are on the arms of a wealthy man. He seems smitten with you. I'm sure he'll buy this sculpture for you. The price is ten thousand."

Gritting my teeth to hold my tongue in I forced a closed mouth smile. I walked away but Heather insisted on keeping me company.

"Is the artist here?" I asked looking around.

"No, he had a family emergency," she informed me. "He goes by a weird name...Rhino. Have you ever heard of him?"

"No I haven't, but he's very talented," I said.

"Yes he is," she said. "He managed to escape the ghetto like Jarvis and become a successful, respectable

African American. It's so hard for young, black men to get out of that life. So many like to make excuses for their failures. It's good to see people like you, Jarvis and others that don't blame slavery for being unfortunate."

My anger ran through me so rapidly I could feel my scalp sweating. This woman was a racist and disrespectful as they come. She felt because I was here amongst the white elitist that she could make such a comment to me. Once again, I thought of Jarvis. I looked over where he stood with two other men. He looked over and winked at me.

"Yes, everyone is responsible for achieving their own success," I said, holding back the vile I felt in my throat.

"Oh my, that is a lovely dress and your butt is sitting up so perfect," said a red-haired white woman that joined us.

"You ever thought of getting some of the fat removed from your behind?" Heather asked. "It would take so much focus off your butt, so people could enjoy how exquisite the dress is on you."

That was it! I couldn't take anymore from her, so I excused myself to go to the restroom. After relieving my bladder, I stood at the sink washing my hands and looking in the mirror at myself. Tears started to fill my eyes because I felt like crap for letting her get away with the things she said to me. I took a deep breath before exiting the restroom. To endure the rest of this evening I needed Heather to stay away from me. It was just my luck to see her standing my Jarvis and a short, brown haired white man. Maybe he just looked short standing next to Jarvis. I wanted to go in the other direction, but Jarvis nodded his head for me to join them. I forced a smile and made my way over.

"Nova, this is my husband, Paul," Heather said smiling as if she didn't just insult me and my people.

"Nice to meet you Nova," Paul said, smiling pleasantly. "Heather told me you're unemployed. Well, that's what this auction is for. We're going to use the money to help African American women with or without kids gain successful employment. I know working at fast foods can't raise a family."

"Jarvis I'm not feeling very well," I said. It wasn't a complete lie. Listening to them was making me nauseous. "You don't have to leave; I'll just catch an uber."

"Nonsense Nova, we can leave," Jarvis said, placing his hand on the small of my back.

"Oh, that's too bad," Heather said sadly. "I had told Jarvis how much you wanted the sculpture we were admiring." I never once told her I wanted that sculpture. There was no way I could attend these events with Jarvis and be his peace and sanity too. He needed me to be his escape from all of this, and I needed to stay strong enough to be there for him. Having to endure repetitive nights like this wasn't possible for me.

When we got back into the limo, Jarvis held my hand, kissing it softly.

"Thank you," he said. "You make these events easier to bear." My intentions were to tell him how I felt about this evening, but I couldn't ruin it for him or us. We were in a good place, so I sucked it up and kept quiet.

A Month Later

Nova

I was so exhausted from spending all day at the Minding My Business pop-up tent event I hosted. The participation was awesome, not to mention I sold every facial cream, body scrub, and herbal blends I had. I'd been to four events selling my products in the last two months, but this one was the first one I hosted. I knew a lot of vendors only participated because of my relationship with Jarvis, but I didn't use his influence in any way to promote it. It had been so much fun being out of the house and interacting with so many different people. Outside of going to events with Jarvis and the few events I attended to sell my products, I was home with him day and night. We were so engrossed with each other in our own little world. Our energies intertwined so strong that sometimes it scared me. My soul was consumed by his energy; he poured into me. I was so deep into him that I had started to reflect him. Sometimes that wasn't a good thing, because Jarvis was still holding a piece of himself so deep inside. It felt like he was battling something within himself and I didn't know how to reach that part of him.

"You okay?" Amoy asked as I pulled up to her beautiful home.

She and Cache had come along to help me with the event. I had already dropped Cache off and was speeding to get Amoy home. All I wanted was to soak in a coconut milk bath and climb into bed. I wished Jarvis was home to put me to sleep but he wasn't due home for a couple of hours. He was hoping to gain another investor, and I'd been praying he sealed the deal.

"Yea, just tired," I replied.

"Come on, talk. You always listening and advising me and Cache. It's your time to vent," she said smiling at me. She was right. I'd never talked to anyone about things that bothered me. Honestly, up until being back with Jarvis, I didn't have any concerns. My life was carefree. Now I was being devoured by a love that was changing me. Change could be good, but I was feeling like I was changing to be in Jarvis' life. I'd never been the person that changed to be accepted by anyone.

"You ever loved someone so much that you feel like you're losing who you are?" I asked.

"You're not happy with Jarvis?" she asked sadly. "You know what. Don't answer that yet. We need some wine with this conversation."

We went inside and Amoy opened a bottle of wine I had given her. Dak had taken the kids to Chucky Cheese so we were alone in the house.

"So, are you happy with him?" she asked again as we sat comfortably in the den.

"That's the problem, Amoy. I'm utterly and completely happy with him but I'm not happy with the life I have with him," I admitted solemnly.

A frown instantly appeared on Amoy's face.

"Is he cheating on you?" she asked.

"No and he would never do that. Amoy, I'm so simple. My life has always been stress-free; my only purpose was to stay true to myself and live a peaceful, happy life," I said. "I'm not living that anymore. I'm so consumed with making Jar's life happy that I'm not living the life I wanted for myself."

"I know you hate going to all the fancy dinners and events. Most of those people are snobs," she said. "Nova, you can still support him and be yourself. Don't change who you are for him or anyone else. Jarvis fell in love with the simple Nova. He's going to love you regardless."

"He's working so hard trying to get enough investors. I'm his escape from all of that, so I just do what I can to keep him sane," I said.

"But what is he doing to make sure you're happy, Nova?" she asked. "I know none of the materialistic shit means anything to you. I've noticed how you've been dressing lately, and you look weird as fuck in those clothes. Be you, don't fake who you are for those people."

Amoy had no idea that Jarvis was faking himself. So many times I've watched him sit quietly in rage as his colleagues belittled him nicely with their privileged attitudes as if they were the reason he was such an accomplished man. Jarvis didn't need any of them to be great. He just needed to realized that within himself

When my phone rang, I quickly answered seeing Jarvis' name come on the screen. He had to be home, because he never called me when he was out of town.

Nona Day   Over You

"I've been calling your phone. We're going to be late for the Governor's dinner party. Where da fuck you at, Nova?" he asked angrily.

There was no way I was playing nice with a bunch of Republicans tonight, and it appalled me that Jarvis wanted to go. Well, he didn't want to go, but one of his black investors was a Republican.

"I'm exhausted Jarvis," I said softly. "I've been at the pop-up tent event all day. I'll just make sure I'm awake when you get home."

"Get damn dress Nova and meet me there," he said, ending the call.

By the time I had left Amoy's house, the wine had given me too much courage. If Jarvis wanted me by his side so damn bad tonight, he was going to have to settle for Nova Lee Champagne, not Jarvis' date. I was in no mood to pretend to be someone I wasn't. When I got home, I dressed to my likeness with my kinky, curly mane flowing freely. My long sleeve maxi dress was a patchwork of white, black, green, purple, yellow, red, orange and beige colors. I wore bright yellow socks with a pair of white shoes with a little black bow on them. I had to admit I only wore the overexaggerated style to piss Jarvis off.

Nona Day   Over You

When I walked into the ballroom, all eyes landed on me. I walked in like I was the queen of the ball with my head held high and my crown standing tall. I could hear whispers coming from people asking who I was, but I ignored them all.

I spotted Jarvis sitting at a table with a few of his colleagues. One couple I was quite familiar with because I'd seen them at previous events. The other two couples I didn't recognize. When he looked up and spotted me coming in his direction, I almost ran out of the building. He was livid but he held a poker face. As I got closer to him I could feel his raging energy inside of me.

"I'm sorry; I think you have the wrong table," a tall, brown-skinned woman said, turning her nose up at me. Jarvis surprised me by standing up and greeting me with a kiss on the cheek. He pulled out my chair for me to sit next to him as he introduced me to everyone.

"Are you coming from a costume party?" Priscilla, the white woman sitting next to her black husband, asked.

"Now, that hurt my feelings, Priscilla. I put a lot of thought into putting this ensemble together," I said jokingly.

Nona Day   Over You

"You're fuckin' drunk," Jarvis whispered in my ear. With a smile on my face, I winked at him.

"Nova, it's good to see you again. I've been wanting to tell you how much I loved the herbal tea blend. I'm more than willing to pay for the next batch," Camille said. Camille was the only female I had previously met. We hit it off good, so I gifted her a basket of some of my products.

"Nova sells herbs and facial products. She's just coming from the first pop-up tent event she hosted," Jarvis said proudly. "A lot of eccentric people buy her items, so she dresses the part."

As if I was a project or deal he had to sell to them, he made sure to let them know I had a master's degree. He had no clue about eccentric people, because he didn't have a clue about who I was. All he knew was that being with me made him happy. And that was all that mattered to him. It infuriated me; he was trying to make excuses for who I was.

"Oh ok, so you have your own company?" Charlotte, the tall, brown-skinned snob, asked.

"No, I don't have time to run a company," I answered.

"Well, what do you do with your time?" Priscilla asked.

"Most of the time, I'm either sitting my ass on Jarvis' lap or laying on my back," I said smiling, staring at Priscilla. "Whichever he prefers."

Camilla and her husband couldn't hold their laughter. Everyone else at the table looked disgusted.

"What da fuck, Nova?" Jar asked angrily. The old Jar was rearing his head, so I contemplated pushing him over the edge. That was just how furious I was at him for lying about my clothes. I didn't care how mad he was, because I was just as angry. He was saved by Camille complimenting all the items I had given her.

"I love that hair. What kind of weave is that?" Priscilla asked.

"It's called natural hair from my scalp. Thank you," I said without a smile. I know you can't tell a wig from natural hair these days, but it irritated me when people were bold enough to ask that question as if black women couldn't possibly have hair like mine. I redirected my conversation to Camille. I could feel Jarvis fuming as he sat beside me.

"That tattoo on your neck looks like it hurts," Priscilla said, referring to my name written through a champagne glass. "I could never do that to my body."

"But you have no problem risking cancer for your tan?" I asked. Her mouth fell open.

"That's enough, Nova," Jarvis said angrily.

"That's okay, Jarvis," Priscilla said with a smirk at me.

Everyone started making small talk again. Jarvis never placed his hand on my thigh. He looked sad and angry at the same time. I started to regret my behavior. The remainder of the evening, I sat quietly while Jarvis conversed with everyone. Camille and her husband were the only ones that showed interest in my presence. Not even Jarvis acknowledged me, not even with a hand on my thigh.

*****

I rode shot gun as Jarvis drove my car home, and Bahka drove the limo home. I tried apologizing to him, but he said nothing. We were falling apart, and I didn't know how to fix us because I didn't know how to fix me. The person I loved most was embarrassed and ashamed of me and my actions. All I wanted him to do was acknowledge me without the facade. When we got home, Jarvis went upstairs. I waited a few minutes before following him. I peeled off my clothes as I made my way to the bedroom. If he wouldn't accept my apology verbally, I'd try asking for forgiveness sexually. It was only a temporary fix to our problem, but I needed to ease his anger and the tension between us.

My heart dropped to the floor when I walked in the bedroom. Jarvis had pulled out his luggage and was throwing clothes in it. Not my clothes...*his clothes.*

"Jarvis, I said I was sorry," I pleaded with him. Still not a word from him. He wouldn't even look at me. "Jarvis, please talk to me."

I was pulling out every piece of clothing he threw in the suitcase and begging for his forgiveness. He finally stopped and stared at me with fire in his eyes.

"Four mothafuckin' investors is all I need. Two of them was sitting at the damn table," he said, walking up on me. "Yo ass come there with that weird ass shit on and talking out the side of yo long ass damn neck cost me those two investors."

Tears started to well up in my eyes. "I'm so sorry."

"Sorry ain't gon' fix this shit, Nova. Put on some damn clothes, because sex ain't fixing this shit either," he said angrily. He chuckled. "Actually you did fix this. I wanted you back here to get over you. I damn sho don't want you in my life now. The foul shit you did, knowing what I wanted and how much it meant to me, helped me get da fuck over yo weird ass."

All I could do was stand there with tears running down my face. I watched him walk over to the mini safe in the living area of the bedroom and take some papers from it. He walked over to the dresser, placed the papers on the dresser and nodded his head for me to come over to him. I walked over with my head hanging low.

"Sign them," he said, placing a pen beside the papers.

"What are they for?" I asked, looking up at him. He demanded I signed them with a bark so deep it echoed through the bedroom. The roar that came from his gut made me sign the papers without reading them. My eyes were so blurry from my tears the only word I remember seeing was ownership. Maybe he was signing over the title to my car. I guess that was my parting gift. After I signed the papers, I looked up at him wanting an explanation for what I signed.

"I didn't buy this house for Valentine or myself," he said. "Do you know why I bought it, Nova?"

"No," I said softly.

"I liked the house, but it was too big for just me. But when I walked out and saw the acres of nothing but green grass and trees all I thought of was you. I visualized you planting shit and doing what you loved to do, but I never imagined I'd actually get to see you in that backyard. Now, that I have, I don't want it. I don't want to be connected to anything that will stop me from getting over you. The house is yours. You can paint the bitch with psychedelic colors and decorate it with ugly ass furniture for all I care."

He reached in the top dresser drawer and pulled out a little black box. A lump big enough to cut off my breath formed in my throat as he sat the box on top of the papers. All I could do was stare at it.

"Sell the bitch if you want," he said before walking out the bedroom. It felt as if my heart had stopped and I couldn't breathe. I wanted to run after him and beg for his forgiveness, but he had drained me of all my energy. My legs were too weak to hold me up, so I flopped down to the floor bawling. I was so broken I couldn't cry out loud. He was over me and us.

Jarvis

I sat in the back of the limo with my luggage just staring at the house. The look on her face when I walked away was enough to break me into a million pieces. I contemplated going back inside to try and be the man she wanted me to be, but I didn't know how to be him without failing at achieving my goals. Going back inside and becoming the man she needed me to be would mean walking away from everything I needed for myself.

The partition came down pulling me from my thoughts.

"Long trip this time? Damn nigga, you just came back," Bahka said, looking at me through the rearview mirror.

"I'm over this shit with her," I said, trying to convince myself. "I'm moving back into the condo."

He raised a brow at me.

"You get a chance at one great love. Everything after that is mediocre shit," Bakha said. "I'll burn Atlanta to the ground before I let any amount of money, power or respect take that type of love from me. Don't be a fool."

"Mothafucka, I pay you to drive me, not advise me," I said angrily. "Now drive."

I didn't need a philosophical love speech telling me I wouldn't ever love like this again. The feeling in the pit of my stomach told me that. I watched the house until it was out of my sight. The more I thought about life without her the more nauseous I became. My mouth started to water, and I could feel myself getting ready to vomit.

"You one stubborn ass nigga," Bahka said, shaking his head.

"Pull da fuck over!" I demanded. He slammed on the brakes. I opened the door and emptied my stomach until nothing, but water came out. Bahka sat in the front seat laughing like shit was funny.

"Now that's what you call lovesick," he said laughing. I closed the door and laid my head back. I couldn't even close my eyes without seeing her face. Not her peaceful beautiful face, but the broken, unhappy face that was my fault. I had been responsible for hurting so many people. Maybe it was best if I stayed away from everyone.

SOUL Publications

Nona Day   Over You

Bahka drove me to my condo playing love songs. If I had a gun on me, I would've put a bullet in his whooper head. By the time I made it to the condo, Amoy was calling my phone. Nova had to have called her and told her what happened. I was in no mood to hear her shit tonight, so I turned my phone off.

About an hour later, I sat at my condo drowning myself in vodka and suffocating in weed. Neither drug was numbing the agony inside of me. She was my morphine. Her love was the only thing that kept me sane. The way she looked at me and the melody of my name coming from her lips was a natural high that no drug could fix. Walking away from her was the hardest thing I'd ever had to do next to seeing dirt thrown on my parents' graves. It wasn't my anger that made me walk away from her. It was finally realizing how unhappy she was with me. I had no clue how to make Nova happy in my life. Hell, I wasn't even happy in my own life. She didn't deserve to be with someone like me. I didn't know how to love her, because I didn't love the person I was, outside of being with her.

When I heard loud banging on the front door, I immediately jumped up thinking it was Nova. The joy and pounding in my heart quickly faded away, because Nova knew nothing about my condo. We had only spent time together at my old condo that I had sold. It wasn't used for cheating on her. I used it for drunken nights when I wasn't able to make it home. I had to uphold the perfect image, so I used my condo to drown myself in liquor and weed. Nova hated seeing me so drunk that I passed out, so sometimes I stayed at the condo. Other times, I just had to be near her, so I would still go home but never in the bedroom with her.

I looked at the security app on my phone to see Amoy standing on the other side of the door. The look on her face let me know she was heated. Her banging went unanswered until I couldn't take it anymore. I walked over and let her inside. The moment she stepped inside she started her rant. Making my way to the sofa, I sat down and laid my head back.

"Jarvis, do you hear me?" she asked furiously.

"Yea," I replied dryly. I did hear everything she said, and I had no argument for her. It was wrong of me to bring Nova back in my life only to hurt her. Yea, with all the money and power I had my life was still a mess. Yea, I needed to seek some kind of help to get myself right. Yea, I kept doing dumb shit. Everything she said was the truth, but the more she talked the angrier I got.

"Shut da fuck up, Amoy!" I roared, making her jump back. I stared at her walking up on her. "Yea, I'm a gah-damn mental, heartless, mothafucka. So, right now ain't the time to fuck with me."

Her eyes grew as big as the moon.

"A-Are you threatening me?" she asked. There it was. The look that she gave me when she found out I killed Aunt Belle. The pity, shame, and hate all resurfaced in her eyes. My own sister could never love me the same as she once did, so I knew I wasn't deserving of Nova's love.

"Get out, Amoy," I said, walking away.

As I slammed the bathroom door, she slammed the front door and left. After taking a cold shower, I set things up in the bedroom and made a call. I lost two possible investors tonight, and it wasn't because of Nova's appearance. Even though, she was wrong as hell for showing up the way she did. Nova had taken as much as she could trying to fit into my life. She had finally reached her breaking point.

"Hi," Charlotte said answering my call.

"Bring your partner and come to my condo," I said ending the call.

Thirty minutes hadn't passed before Charlotte and Priscilla were walking inside my condo. Yea, I had fucked both of them a few times before Nova came back in my life. These were the bitches that cost me their husbands' partnership. Charlotte and Priscilla weren't bothered by Nova's appearance. They hated her for her place in my life, so they set out to embarrass her. Their plan to make me dismiss Nova didn't work, so they *advised* their husbands not to invest with me.

"Take off your clothes and go upstairs. Go ahead and get started without me," I said lighting a blunt. They wasted no time peeling off their clothes right in the living room.

"I knew she couldn't keep you satisfied for too long," Priscilla said smiling at me. This loose pussy bitch didn't know how murderous I was feeling right now. If one more disrespectful thing came out their mouths about Nova, I was shipping their asses back to their husbands in body parts. Fuck the new Jarvis. The old Jarvis was back in full effect and ready to make shit happen. Mothafuckas didn't appreciate me being nice.

Ten minutes later, I walked in on Priscilla eating Charlotte out. My dick couldn't even get hard. They ate each other out before they started using the toys on the bed.

They were giving each other multiple orgasms and yet my dick was still soft.

"When are you going to join us?" Priscilla asked, staring at me and licking her lips.

"Do y'all know your dry pussy, silicone breast, mayonnaise ass and muscle ass bitches caused me to lose the best thing in my life?" I asked. Priscilla's ass was flat and couldn't get wet for shit, but she could suck a dick. Charlotte's pussy was good but was muscular like a dude.

"Jarvis, you don't have to be so mean. We'll make sure our husbands invest with you," Charlotte said. "We just didn't like you flaunting trash in our face."

A loud yelp came from both of them when I pointed my gun at Charlotte's forehead and clicked it. Tears immediately started to fall from their eyes.

"Now, say one mo' gah-damn negative thing about her," I dared them. They cried, apologized and pleaded for their lives.

I walked over and grabbed the remote off the nightstand and turned the television on. Their eyes nearly popped out their heads when they saw themselves on the seventy-inch television hanging on the wall.

Nona Day   Over You

"W-what are you going to do with that?" Priscilla asked anxiously.

"Nothing, as long as I get a call from your husbands in the next two days agreeing to invest with me," I said giving them an evil grin. "Now get da fuck out my shit."

As Priscilla and Charlotte were getting dressed and sobbing softly, Amoy came back banging at my door again. I couldn't understand why she didn't just use the damn doorbell. She really wanted to see my ugly side tonight. If that was what she wanted, I was in the mood to give it to her. When I opened the door, my heart stopped, eyes opened like a full moon, and the world shifted but not in my favor. Our eyes pierced through each other. Nova stood there with bloodshot, swollen eyes full of tears. She looked so fragile, scared and heartbroken. She opened her mouth to speak but broke our gaze and looked over my shoulder. The way she stared at me with pure disgust in her eyes sent a chilling bolt of fear through my core. Walking away from her was hard, but to see the revulsion in her eyes for me was unbearable. The tears in her eyes started to fall as she stood with her bottom lip trembling. The shock of seeing the two women that tried to tear her down in my apartment had to be enough to make her hate me forever, but I couldn't allow that to happen. Nova finally found the strength to turn and run away, but I yanked her up and threw her over my shoulder.

"Get da fuck out!" I demanded to Priscilla and Charlotte as I carried Nova kicking and screaming to one of the three bedrooms in the condo. The language and names she called me were unbelievable.

I pleaded with her to calm down so I could explain, but she was hysterical. She fought with every fiber in her being to get away from me. To hear her screaming the words I hate you was beyond painful. Her tiny fists punched me, and her nails dug into my face, but I couldn't let her go. Not this way. Not with her thinking what she was thinking. The louder she screamed for me to let her go, the tighter I held her, begging for the chance to explain. I don't know how long we tussled before her small frame finally lost all the strength it had to fight me. Her body may've lost strength, but the gut-wrenching cry that came from her caused tears to slip from my tear ducts. She collapsed in my arms like a rag doll and sobbed softly. I slid to the floor with her in my arms rocking her until she fell asleep.

Nova

The sun was shining through the long curtain-free windows. I couldn't believe I was lying in bed with him. It was a relief when I realized we both were still fully clothed. He held me in his arms with my head on his chest. Everything felt so right being wrapped up in his arms, but nothing was right. I wasn't right for enjoying having him hold me. My soul was so consumed with love for this man that the thought of not having him in my life terrified me. There was love and then there was life altering, soul snatching, breathless love that made your heart feel as if it would combust. After only a few hours of him walking out on me, I literally felt like I was going to die from a broken heart. When Amoy called and told me where he was, I rushed over to mend us.

But this wasn't right. There was no way we could overcome what I walked in on last night. Here I was thinking those women didn't like me because of who I was. Instead they disliked me because he was having sex with them. My brain was screaming for me to get out of the bed, but my heart and body were relishing in the comfort of his arms. Tears started to fill my eyes because I knew this wasn't right. I had just caught him with not one but two women. He must've felt my body tense up because his arms held me tighter. With my head still on his chest, I could feel his heart pounding rapidly. I closed my eyes tight to fight the tears back.

"Jarvis, please let me go," I pleaded softly. He held me a few seconds longer before slowly releasing his hold on me. Without his arms around me anymore, I still couldn't pull myself away from him. I was so conflicted with the love I had for him. A part of me wanted to walk away from this life with him. The other part of me was willing to endure losing myself to have him in my life.

I slowly pulled myself away from him, and he climbed out the bed along with me. Thoughts of lying in the bed where he's had sexual intercourse with two other women only a few hours ago infuriated me. He was staring at me when I turned around to face him. He stood on the opposite side of the bed.

"How fuckin' dare you lay me in the same bed you fucked other women in hours ago?" I asked angrily. "I've tried to love you the best I could, but you don't deserve me.

Nona Day   Over You

You deserve those types of women. So I'm gon' let you have them. Maybe they can tolerate trying to love you, but I'm done trying. I'm over you and this relationship!"

I went on a rant about how low he was for leaving me to come lay with them. My rage was so high I couldn't even shed another tear. We were so in sync with each other's emotions that he started to feed off my anger. I could see the fury building in his eyes, but at this point I didn't care anymore.

"Well, what da fuck you came here for?" he asked, walking toward me. "That shit was settled when I left the damn house!"

"Because my stupid ass thought we were worth saving," I replied. "Only person worth saving in this relationship is me."

"Well, get da fuck out!" He demanded furiously.

I stormed out of the bedroom and made my way downstairs with Jarvis behind me.

"Yo ass always talking about how snobbish and judgmental people with money are, but yo ass ain't no damn better, Nova. You think just because you don't live your life being motivated by money or power that you somehow better than people that do. Your meaning of success ain't no mothafuckin' golden rule to having a happy life," he said, walking behind me.

I turned around to face him before opening the front door.

"Maybe it isn't but lying about who you are to be accepted by people for money and power damn sure isn't. I'll stay broke as hell before I live a miserable ass life like you just for shit that I can't take with me when I leave this earth," I said.

I turned back around and opened the door. Amoy and Dak were standing on the other side. Amoy's solemn face and swollen eyes caused my soul to ache for her. Dak stood by her side holding her hand with an intense look on his face. I stepped to the side to let them in keeping my eyes on Amoy. She looked so broken my eyes started to tear up for whatever pain she was feeling.

"Gah-damn, Amoy! I ain't in the mood for yo judgmental shit!" Jarvis said angrily.

"Chill man, we need to talk," Dak said, stepping in Jarvis' space.

"Oh, she brought you here because she thinks I threatened her? Nigga, you bleed like me," Jarvis said staring at Dak. Jarvis was on the edge ready to jump off.

"Nigga, Brandon dead," Dak said through gritted teeth. My eyes immediately zoomed in on Jarvis. He stood there studying Dak's face as if he was trying to understand what he had just said. I could hear soft sobs coming from Amoy, so I walked over and wrapped my arms around her and cried with her. Brandon was like their little brother. Jarvis made sure to keep him out of the streets by paying his way through college. Brandon wanted to be an engineer and Jarvis was going to make sure he became one. Jarvis spoiled Brandon as long as he stayed in school.

When reality finally hit Jarvis, he walked over and flopped down on the sofa with his head down. I wanted to go to him, but he was in a messed-up place right now. Dak walked over and sat on the loveseat across from the sofa. Amoy and I stopped crying long enough to join them in the living room. Amoy sat next to Dak while I eased down beside Jar praying he didn't push me away. He quickly looked up at me with the most hopeless eyes I had ever seen. I held his hand and squeezed it as tight as I could. He needed to know I was here for him.

"What happened?" Jar asked, dropping his head again.

"He got jacked leaving the club last night. Nobody talking though," Dak replied. Jarvis lifted his head, tilted it and stared at Dak.

"So we don't know who did it?" Jarvis asked. Dak shook his head.

"Jarvis, the police are looking into it," she told at him.

"Somebody gon' tell me something," Jarvis said quickly standing up.

"Where you going?" I asked following Jarvis to the front door, but he ignored me.

"To fuck his life up," Dak said, standing up.

"Please don't let him do anything stupid," Amoy pleaded with Dak.

"Stay here with Nova. Cache and Noble got the kids," Dak told Amoy. He left out the condo behind Jarvis.

"What is he going to do?" I asked worriedly.

"I need a drink," Amoy said, walking past me and into the kitchen. I followed her to the kitchen and back into the living room. She carried a bottle of cognac while I carried two glasses.

"I'm so sorry about what happened to Brandon. He was nice to me and made me laugh," I said, remembering the times he would be at Jarvis' old condo with us.

Amoy started reminiscing by talking about Brandon while wiping her tears away. I listened to her pour her heart out about Brandon until she fell asleep. Sleep had abandoned me because I was so worried about Jarvis. He was with Dak, but it didn't stop me from worrying. I needed to calm my nerves, so I went searching for weed in the condo. I was sure Jarvis had some in there. When I walked into what had to be the master bedroom, I got sick to my stomach. The messy bed had sex toys on it. Quickly closing the room door, I wanted to run back to Dothan as fast as I could. Looking at Amoy sound asleep stopped me from leaving. I couldn't leave her here alone, so I went into the bedroom where I slept earlier and climbed into bed.

I gasped for my breath when I awoke to Jarvis hovering over me on all fours. His face held no emotion. His eyes looked lifeless. There was a bruise on his upper right jaw and a few specks of blood on his shirt. I wondered if he was fighting Dak or Brandon's killer. Whoever it was

I was sure they were dead. I laid there holding my breath waiting for him to speak.

"I used to fuck them, but I haven't put my dick in another female since you came back," he explained. I listened as he told me why the women were at his condo. A huge weight lifted from my chest knowing he didn't have sex with them.

"You have blood on your shirt," I said. I didn't want to discuss last night. My only concern was his mental and emotionally well-being right now. He lifted up, resting on his knees and pulled his shirt over his head. "You look so tired."

He lowered his body, lying flat on top of me with his head on my chest. I opened my legs to let his body rest comfortably against mine. He started to relax as I gently massaged his head, shoulders and back. This was one of those moments where all he needed to feel was our connection. Sex wasn't his concern. I started humming a soft melody to soothe his stress away. We both drifted off to sleep.

I was awakened with the touch of his hand sliding under my blouse sending tingling sensations through my body. His touch alone caused my pulse to vibrate inside my core. My blouse slowly lifted until the touch of his hands were replaced with his wet tongue caressing my belly. His hand traveled to my breasts and started massaging them. He looked up at me asking for permission with his eyes. I reached down and unfastened my jeans. He removed my jeans while I pulled my blouse over my head. The yearning inside me couldn't resist his touch. I wanted him as much as he needed me.

After removing my jeans and panties, he dipped his head between my opened thighs. His warm breath against my hot, wet flower caused my body to shudder. Sliding his arms under my thighs, he spread them wide, lifting them in the air. His tongue parted my lower lips like the Red Sea

"Jarvis," I moaned, arching my back and throwing my head back. His tongue was gentle, precise, sensual and erotic. I didn't know if I was inebriated from the tongue lashing he was giving me, but it felt as if it was scripting my name and I love you with a gel tip pen between my folds. My hips twirled with the slow rhythm of his tongue strokes. I could hear him slurping and sucking my juices. My body nearly lifted off the bed when he started pulverizing my swollen bud with his tongue. I gripped the back of his head burying his face against my mound. A rush of fluid splashed from me as I cried out his name. He licked, slurped and sucked me from front to back until I was coming again. I collapsed shivering while my heated body was dripping wet from sweat. Jarvis placed soft wet kisses starting at the top of my toes and stopping with a kiss on my third eye.

Over A Week Later

Jarvis had been a walking zombie since Brandon's death. After the night at his condo, he showed no emotion and looked like a bum. Colleagues and business partners were calling his phone, because he wasn't going to work, attending meetings or events. He wasn't drinking or smoking. His spirit was dead inside him and I had no clue how to reach him. I tried talking to him, but he wouldn't open up to me. Word on the streets was he was terrorizing everybody to find out who killed Brandon. This was the Jarvis that I hadn't seen after I left Atlanta. He was slowly dying on the inside.

Today was Brandon's funeral. Jarvis showed up late in jeans and a T-shirt. Completely sober, he sat in the back of the church silently. He only stayed long enough to give his condolences to Brandon's' father. After the funeral, I went to the condo to check on him, but he wasn't there. His phone kept going to voicemail, so I finally gave up and went back to the house. I had plans of moving out of Jarvis' house, because this wasn't a home without him. Him signing over the house meant nothing to me because I didn't need this house without him. I was shocked to see his Tesla parked in front of the house, but relieved. This was the first time he'd been here since he moved out. Most of my time was spent at the condo with him or worrying about him.

Binx came rushing down the stairs when I came through the door. I was so wrapped up in Jarvis' life, I wasn't only neglecting my life, but Binx also. I picked him up and he purred against me. He jumped out my arms and ran up the stairs. Jarvis must've been upstairs in the bed. I giggled because Binx wanted me to throw Jarvis out of the bed. When I walked into the room, Jarvis was sitting on side of the bed rolling a blunt. Binx stood by me looking at Jarvis.

"That damn cat evil, Nova," Jarvis said staring at Binx.

"He doesn't like you because he knows you don't like him," I said.

"Well, we going on a date and his bitch ass can't come," he said, standing up. With the blunt in his hand, he grabbed two from the nightstand. "Meet me in the backyard in fifteen minutes."

He walked out of the room leaving me puzzled. I didn't know how to dress for our date and wondered why I was meeting him in the backyard. I slipped on a pair of yoga shorts and a T-shirt after stripping out of the funeral outfit I wore. I wanted to ask him how I needed to dress for our date. I made my way downstairs and to the sliding door by the pool. After walking around the pool and outside shower, I stepped out on the lawn. My heart absolutely melted. There was a campfire and a picnic blanket. He had done the most amazing thing by having a gigantic projection screen with the original *Steel Magnolias* playing. He stood by the picnic blanket waiting for me to join him. I couldn't stop the tears from falling as I walked toward him.

"Jarvis, I love this," I said looking around at the thoughtful set up.

"You always talking about going camping, moonlight dinners and drive-in movies. So I gave it to you all in one package," he said with a straight face. I couldn't remember the last time I'd seen him smile, and this beautiful date he planned for us still wasn't enough to make him smile. I tiptoed and met his lips; he allowed me to kiss him softly.

"Thank you so much but you didn't have to do this," I said. With all the pain he'd been feeling with Brandon's death, he had completely shut himself off to me. Even when I tried to comfort him, he showed no interest and pushed me away.. This was the only attention he had given me in the past week.

"Antoine made all the food. I supplied all the weed," he said smiling. "Come on. Let's sit down and see what this corny ass movie is about."

We sat down on the blanket.

"It's kinda sad. With everything that has happened I don't think this is the best movie to watch," I told him. He looked disappointed but used a remote to turn the projector off. I crawled over and straddled his lap, taking the blunt from his hand. "Let's just enjoy each other's company."

I inhaled as long as I could before nodding my head for him to take my shotgun. He tilted his head and slightly opened his mouth. My body shivered at the brush of my lips against his while I released the smoke into his mouth. He placed his hand in the back of my head and covered my mouth with his. We moaned as our tongues battled in each other's mouths. He took the blunt from my hand and put it out. His masculine hands groped my butt cheeks and I started humping the bulge in his jeans. My wetness started to saturate through my yoga shorts. Just as I was getting ready to explode on his lap, his phone rang. I stopped, so he could answer it.

"Don't fuckin' stop! Keep going. You look sexy as fuck hunching me," Jarvis said, tasting and biting on my neck. I did as he ordered until my nectar gushed onto his lap. He wrapped his arms around my waist, and I collapsed resting my head on his shoulder.

"Thank you," I murmured while trying to catch my breath.

"For what?" he asked.

I lifted my head from his shoulder and kissed him softly.

"For thinking of me through your heartache. I don't know the pain you feeling from losing Brandon, but I'm here for you, Jarvis. You don't have to go through this alone." There was an uncertainty in his eyes that didn't sit well in my spirit. I gently held his face between my hands. "You know that, right?"

For a brief second all that could be heard were the sounds of crickets.

"You left me, Nova," he said, staring at me. The agony in his voice crushed me.

"I didn't know you wanted me to stay," I explained, gently holding his face between my hands.

"I didn't damn want you to stay. I needed yo ass here," he said with a scowl on his face. He was still angry with me and I didn't understand why. All he had to do was ask me to stay before I left for Dothan and I never would've left. I wanted to get angry with him, but I decided this was a moment for understanding.

"I thought about you every day. So many times I picked up my phone to call you, but I thought I didn't matter to you," I said. "My heart couldn't handle more rejection from you."

"Don't leave me again or I'm not gon' be nice when I drag yo ass back the next time," he said sternly. I laughed even though I knew he was dead serious. "Now, get yo freaky ass off me. Nigga trying to have a nice romantic evening with yo ass and you hunching me and busting nuts all over my jeans."

I laughed hysterically as I climbed off his lap. He grabbed his phone and immediately stood up.

"Come on. I gotta go handle something," he said. I didn't ask any questions as I followed him inside the house. He showered and dressed in black jeans and a hoodie.

"Jarvis, please be careful," I said before he walked out of the bedroom. Instead of looking at me, he looked at Binx who was sitting in the middle of the bed.

"Make sho that mothafucka ain't in the bed when I come back," he said staring Binx down. When Binx jumped off the bed, Jarvis jumped with fear. Binx scurried out of the bedroom. I looked at Jarvis trying to hold in my laughter. He was truly scared of a little black cat.

"I'm getting a pit bull. Let's see how bad his ass is then," he said. He walked over and kissed me on the forehead before leaving the house.

Jarvis

"You sure about this?" I asked the young dude that had disrespected Nova at the club. I had put out an anonymous hundred grand reward for information about Brandon's murder. He didn't have the murderer, but he had located the Ferrari that was stolen from Brandon. The niggas that killed him left his body on side of the damn street like he was trash. There was no way I could walk away and just grieve his death. Someone had to pay for his life with their life.

"I'm positive. I doubt they the ones that did it, but they got the car in there," he said. We were posted across the street from the warehouse.

"How many in there?" I asked.

"Niggas been coming and going, so I'm not sure. The owner usually closes up about midnight," he informed me. "He usually walks out with two bodies around him. I guess he worried somebody gon' rob him."

Nona Day   Over You

I stared at the kid. He reminded me of Brandon as he stood tall by my side. There was something about him that told me he wasn't a street kid. But I didn't trust anyone, and he was no exception.

"How I know you didn't do it and sell the car to them?" I asked. "You might be scared they gon' rat you out."

He held a straight face and stared over at the building.

"I didn't personally know Brandon, but I've seen him around the clubs a few times. Everybody knew he was connected to you…I mean the old you, Jarhead, so that gave him respect," he said. "But I could tell by the way he carried his self that shit meant nothing to him. He was always chilled and humble. A nigga like me would've took that connection status and acted a damn fool with it."

Brandon was a humble kid that wanted more than a street life. He never let peer pressure, or his upbringing deter him from what he wanted. When I was down and out bad, he made sure to come check on me every day. Sometimes he would just sit there knowing I didn't want to talk. Other times, he would act like a clown just to make me laugh. All he ever talked about was making his father, Amoy and me proud of him. He had already made us proud by following his dreams. Once again, I lost my chance to tell someone how much they meant to me.

"You know you only get half since they aren't the actually killers?" I asked staring at him.

"I don't want the money. I just want whoever killed him to pay," he said. I stared at him for a few minutes. He finally looked at me.

"Y'all was lovers or something?" I asked. "I mean that's cool if y'all was. I ain't homophobic."

"What?" he asked shocked. "Hell no! Man, why da fuck you ask me something like that?"

I had to laugh at myself. "My bad, dog. I guess I watch too much Law and Order."

He chuckled and shook his head.

"I ain't no killer but I can look out for you," he said.

"Nah, you don't need to know shit about this. Gone home. I'll make sure you get paid for what you did whether you want it or not," I told him, holding out my hand. He nodded his head and shook my hand.

After the kid left, I posted up before I made my move. I walked up to the closed warehouse and banged on the roll up door. When I didn't get an answer, I tried my luck. I bent down and tried pushing the door up. It shocked me when the door came up. These simple-minded fools didn't have the door locked. The loud music was the reason my banging went unheard.

"What da fuck?" One big nigga said, walking toward me with his hand behind him. I didn't give him the chance to pull out his gun before sending one to his dome. I stepped over his body and two more came rushing toward me. I laid one down with two holes to his head. The last clown standing didn't have a gun.

"Jarhead?" he asked trying to recognize me with my hoodie over my head. I pulled it off, so he could see it was me.

"All I wanna know is who brought the car to you," I lied. As soon as I got the information I wanted he was dead too. Everyone in Atlanta knew who this car belonged to because of his connection to me. To buy this car knowing it was stolen was disrespectful to me.

"A nigga they call Frito," he blabbed. "He stay in Grove Park. I think you used to fuck his bitch. Her name Vickie."

Nona Day   Over You

I put two in his head and walked out the warehouse, making a call to Noble for a cleanup crew. I hadn't killed anyone in over a year, and it felt different this time. There was a time when I felt nothing after a kill. I felt remorse and regret this time, but this was a necessary deed; it had to be done. Three murders and one more to go.

I went to the condo, took a shower and dressed in a black Armani suit, white button-down shirt and blue and white striped tie. A pair of Versace loafers were on my feet. It was almost two o'clock in the morning when I found Frito. He had pulled into an apartment complex, and a few corner boys were posted up trying to make some bread. When he stepped out his car, I stepped out of mine and called his name. He laughed hysterically as he approached me.

"Ain't this bout a bitch," Frito said still laughing. When we were eye to eye, he stopped laughing as we stared each other down. "Y'all come check y'all street legend out."

The group of young boys walked over to us.

"You killed Brandon?" I asked calmly.

"If I did, what you gon' do about it?" he asked. "You ain't bout to kill me right here. You ain't shit to the streets no more in your expensive clothes. Yo ass throw money to the place that taught you the game and run off to socialize with yo rich friends."

"Did you kill Brandon?" I repeated even though I was seething with anger inside. I wanted to snap his neck right there in the parking lot. The only thing that stopped me was Nova. I had done so much dirt and didn't give a damn about being caught. Now, I had a reason to care.

"And again, what you gon' do about it?" he asked with his head tilted. All the young dudes stood around waiting for my reply.

"I'm not going to do anything. It's against my street cred to snitch, so I just wanna know. I'll let karma handle you. Brandon didn't deserve that shit," I said.

"Y'all witnessing y'all weak ass legend. This nigga in my hood in a suit wanting me to admit to some shit," he said, looking at the young boys. They stood there silently shaking their heads. "Some shit he already know the answer to."

I gave him a wicked grin when I saw the red dot on his forehead. The young boys took several steps back while staring at Frito. He didn't understand what was about to happen to him; he looked at the boys cluelessly.

"I'm gon' do for you what you didn't do for Brandon," I said still smiling. He stared at me knowing he had a reason to worry. "Repent."

He looked at the young boys as if he was asking them to explain what was happening. I could smell the fear starting to ooze from his pores. He still had no idea the target was on him, but the tears that filled his eyes told me that he knew it was over for him.

"Come on man," he pleaded standing still. "I have a family to feed. You know how this street shit go."

"Brandon wasn't part of the streets, nigga," I said through gritted teeth. I held up five fingers as each finger went down this punk nigga started to cry still standing stiff as a board. He didn't know how but he knew he was about to die. When my last finger went down, his head exploded like a nine-millimeter firing into a watermelon. Blood splattered all over me before his body slumped to the ground.

"Call 911 and report a murder," I said staring down at Frito's headless body.

"Jarhead, I'll do it, but you need to leave the scene first," one of the boys said. I looked up at him. These young dudes weren't going to say shit about what happened here. Even if they did, nothing could be proven. That's how I moved.

"Nah, I'm good. I don't have a reason to run," I said. He shrugged his shoulders and made the call.

The cops took me down to the station and questioned me. I was a well-respected businessman just tracking leads on his little brother's murder. It wasn't my fault that I was there to witness Frito's murder. Plus, they weren't going to waste man hours and money trying to find out who ended Frito's worthless life. The detectives believed everything I said, so I was released within an hour.

*****

I was surprised to see she wasn't in the bed. Even Binx wasn't sitting on the bed. My heart started to pound thinking she had left me again. I quickly searched the drawers and the closet for her things. I breathed a sigh of relief when I saw everything was there. Then I realized she hated these clothes, so she wouldn't take them. Panic set in again until I looked down and saw the ugly ass shoes of hers. I searched the house but couldn't find her. When Binx came inside through the sliding kitchen door. I walked out into the backyard and made my way inside the greenhouse. She looked up at me with concern.

"I couldn't sleep," she said softly.

"Come on. Let's go to bed," I told her. She peeled off her garden gloves and walked over to me. Just the simple gesture of her holding my hand warmed my entire body.

The next morning I dressed for work. It was time to go back to my regular life. I couldn't deny some of Frito's words cut deep. I didn't regret my accomplishments, but the fact that I was pretending to be someone I wasn't, to satisfy people that didn't give a damn about me, bothered me. It probably wouldn't bother me so much if being the old me didn't bring back so many bad memories. I was torn on the inside and didn't know how to deal with it. The only thing that kept me sane was Nova. The way she loved me was my peace.

Nova was already up and in the kitchen with Antoine talking and laughing. She had on one of her weird ass outfits, and all I could do was smile and shake my head. Her hair was in two long plaits. I walked over, stood behind her and whispered in her ear.

"I want yo hair like this tonight," I said. "I'm gon' use them for saddle reigns when I hit it from the back." Her goofy ass made noises like a horse making me laugh. She turned around to face me.

"Guess what?" she asked excited.

"You pregnant?" I asked, hoping she was. We never discussed kids and I didn't know if she was on birth control or not. She had to be because we fucked raw too much for her not to be pregnant by now.

"No I'm on the pill," she said, gently slapping me on the chest. "An old college friend of mine is opening an herbal tea and coffee shop. He's considering using some of my blends."

"He?" I asked. I didn't doubt her shit was good enough to sell. I just didn't like the thought of her talking to some nigga I didn't know.

"Yes Jarvis. I think the jealousy is cute, but the friendship is platonic," she said smiling at me.

"I still wanna meet him," I said.

"I have no problem with that," she said. "You look sexy wearing suits."

"Well, I'll make sure to wear a tie tonight when I'm digging in your guts," I said, smacking her on the ass. Antoine chuckled. "Now, come walk me to the door."

As she walked me to the door, I listened to her ramble about her plans for the day. All I made out was yoga, the park, greenhouse, and community event. Nova loved volunteering. She had abandoned everything she loved to do to be here with me.. We were so connected to each other that the outside world didn't exist. Now she had started doing the things she used to do.

When I opened the door, Amoy was standing on the other side with a scowl on her face. I knew she must've heard about Frito's murder. The look on her face was full of disappointment, disgust, aggravation and anger. Once again that was the look she gave me when she discovered I killed Aunt Belle. Seeing the look in her face made me wonder what my parents would think of me. I saw so much of our mother in her and wondered would Ma had looked at me the same way. Pops was a smart man and probably would've thought of a better way to handle Aunt Belle's betrayal. He also would've dealt with Frito differently.

"I can't believe you were stupid enough to kill him. You could've been charged for his murder and ruined your life," Amoy said angrily. She walked inside the house and we stood facing each other.

"Well I wasn't, so shut up about it," I said nonchalantly.
Amoy shook her head. "Still doing stupid, reckless stuff that could cost you everything you've built. You'll never change Jarvis."

Every bad choice she felt I made would always remind her of what I did. No matter how hard I tried to prove myself to her, she still held resentment toward me.

"You bust your behind to get where you are only to act like a simple ass thug," Amoy said angrily.

"We can't change what's been done," Nova said, standing beside me. She held my hand which helped calm the anger brewing in me. I didn't want to fight with Amoy anymore. The only thing I wanted to do was prove to her I was worthy of her full forgiveness. "Amoy, Jarvis was on his way to work."

"Yea, I'm leaving," she said. "You need to stop being so damn gullible for him. He's going to get you caught up in some dumb shit Nova."

"Good, and don't bring yo ass back to my house telling me how I should live my life," Jarvis said staring at her. She waved me off and walked toward the front door until I called her name. She turn to face me.

"I mean it. You ain't welcome here or in my damn life," I said. "Don't want you to be associating with a simple ass thug." It wasn't that I didn't want Amoy in my life. I just couldn't stand to see how disappointed she was in me every time I saw her.

"Don't call me when you fuck your entire life up," Amoy said slamming the door on her way out.

"I don't want you spending time with her," I said to Nova.

"Jarvis that's not fair," Nova said sadly. "She's my friend. I'm sure she's only upset because she's worried about you."

"Do what I said," I said sternly. "My own fuckin' blood wants nothing to do with me, so why would you want to deal with her?"

"Jarvis, Amoy loves you," Nova said. "She's just being protective like you've always been for her."

"You see how she looks at me," I said. "That ain't love."

A Month Later

Nova

I climbed out of bed and went to the bathroom to relieve my bladder. So many thoughts were running through my head. The only thing that brought a smile to my face was my meeting with Kendall. We had made a deal to start selling my herbs in his store and they had become a huge success. Kendall and I shared so many interests. We would spend hours together doing things we loved to do. There was no kind of romantic connection between us. I just enjoyed being with someone that considered doing things I liked to do. To keep the peace between us, I did as Jarvis ordered and stayed away from Amoy. We still texted each other, but there was no more wine and weed nights for us. Once again, I was back to being stuck in the house with nothing to do.

Since Frito's murder, Priscilla and Charlotte's husbands declined to invest with him. Jarvis didn't even put up a fight to keep them. They didn't want to be associated with any kind of negativity, and Jarvis' connections to the murder was too suspect for them. There was never an official investigation into the murder, but people talked. Gossip was floating around that Jarvis killed Frito. It didn't take long for that information to get back to his colleagues. After word got out the Jarvis was with Frito when he was murdered, it tainted his squeaky clean image amongst his business associates. He was in a rough neighborhood with a known drug dealer and criminal. That sent him into a downward spiral. Not to mention Amoy chewing him out for choosing to handle Brandon's murderer himself. As of now, they hadn't spoken to each other.. Their intense argument about his hot temper and recklessness was eye opening for me.

After getting dressed, I made my way over to Amoy's office. I only hoped Jarvis wasn't having me followed since he demanded I stay away from Amoy. Amoy had a successful accounting firm, handsome husband and two beautiful babies. It made me wonder if I would ever have that kind of life with Jarvis. I had even tried to have conversations with Jarvis about my herbal business, but it didn't seem to matter to him. He worked nonstop and made no time for us. The only thing he wanted was my love and legs open. Things were changing between us, and I was becoming someone that adapted to the situation I was in. This wasn't the person I wanted to be for me, him or us.

Nona Day   Over You

"I'm so sorry to bother you at work," I said, sitting on the sofa in Amoy's office. "I just really needed to talk."

"What's he done?" she asked, sitting on the sofa with me.

"Amoy, why do you always assume Jarvis has done something wrong?" I asked. "How do you know it's not me that is the problem?"

"Because you're not problematic," she answered with a smile. "Jarvis is my brother and I love him, but I know how he is."

"How is he?" I asked.

She laughed. "You stay with him. You know."

Tears started to well up in my eyes. She didn't know his heart ached for her acceptance. She didn't realize he felt she still resented him for killing Aunt Belle. Nor did she know he ached for his father's forgiveness that he didn't need. I didn't doubt she loved Jarvis and wanted what was best for him, but Amoy's judgmental ways wouldn't allow her to see how broken he was.

"I know that he's hurting and won't open up to me about it. Jarvis is battling within himself and it's tearing him apart. And I'm losing myself trying to help him keep it together," I admitted quickly wiping a lonely tear from my cheek.

"Nova, I'm so sorry," she said, pulling me into her arms. I didn't need her pity. Jarvis needed to know she loved and accepted him regardless of who he was or his past actions.

"I love him, Amoy, but I feel like I'm shrinking in his life," I said breaking our embrace.

"I'll talk to him, Nova. I know he loves you," she said sincerely with tears in her eyes.

"I don't need you to talk to him for me, Amoy. He needs an open and honest conversation with you, about your feelings toward him."

"I don't understand," she said puzzled by my statement.

"He's still holding a lot inside regarding your parents' and Aunt Belle's deaths. He used to share some of his aches with me, but over the last month or so I get nothing. It's like he's dead on the inside, and that's slowly killing me," I said. "Have you forgiven him, Amoy?"

Her eyes grew big. I knew I was probably overstepping my boundaries, but I felt a part of me was connected to their tragedy since I was connected to Jarvis. His well-being affected me. My soul, energy and heart were so connected to Jarvis sometimes I could feel his pain.

"Of course I've forgiven him," she said. "I mean I know I give him a hard time, that's only because I love him. Jarvis has changed his life so much and I'm so proud and happy for him. I know he was more affected by Aunt Belle's death than me, because he's the one that pulled the trigger. I never felt the need to let him know I forgave him, because I understood why he did it."

We were both in full tears by now.

"He doesn't know who he wants to be. He plays the role that he feels everyone accepts but he also doesn't want to be who he was, because he hasn't forgiven himself. In order to balance his life he needs to be honest and open with himself. I can't help him do that because I'm trying to balance myself," I said.

"You mentioned he wants my father's forgiveness," she said. "For what?"

Nona Day   Over You

"Just talk to him, Amoy. And I mean talk with no judgment," I pleaded with her.

"I will. I promise," she said, hugging me again. "Thank you so much for loving him."

After leaving Amoy's office, I felt better. I was there for Jarvis, so I couldn't lay my burdens on him. Being able to talk and let go of my worries helped lift a weight off me. I spent most of the day working on a few virtual jobs. The rest of my day was spent doing yoga and some volunteer work at community centers. I loved doing things that made me feel good about myself on the inside. When I got home, Jarvis was walking out of the front door. He walked up to me as I made my was the front steps and kissed me on the forehead.

"I'll be back later," he said.

"Jarvis, we need to talk," I said.

"We'll talk tonight, Nova," he said. "I ain't got time right now. We got a dinner party to attend tonight. It starts at eight, so make sure you here to get ready."

I didn't know how to feel about my life right now. Everything I did revolved around Jarvis. He was in a fog so thick he was coming and going with no direction. Days would pass and he would just show up like he hadn't been absent from our bed. I played the nurturing, caring mate comforting him whenever he felt lost. He still wouldn't open himself up to me. All I knew was that he loved and needed me in his life. The sad part was the only time I was happy now was when he wasn't around. It broke my heart to feel that way because I loved him so much. Even our sex had become a way for him to relieve stress instead of a way for us to bond and express our love. There were no intimate moments of us connecting with each other and I needed that to be in his life.

I needed a distraction, something I enjoyed doing. When Kendall hit me up to attend a neo-soul lounge, I couldn't resist. Jarvis would just have to attend the dinner party without me. It was time to put myself first.

Later That Evening

When Kendall hit me up to attend a neo-soul lounge, I couldn't resist. Jarvis would just have to attend the dinner party without me. It was time to put myself first.

The live music at the lounge sounded Grammy worthy. The vibe was relaxed and positive. These were the simple things that I missed so much. Kendall didn't tell me it was open mic night and surprised me by having the owner call me to the stage to sing. I wasn't shy about my vocals, so I made my way to the stage. I sang Rihanna's We Found Love with Kendall's help. The evening out was the most fun I'd had in a couple of months.

My joyful evening came crashing down when Jarvis walked in the lounge. He had been calling my phone, but I ignored his calls. It was my plan to deal with him after my great evening out. Now, here he was, acting cool as a cucumber but I could feel his anger with me. I was frozen as he approached the small round table that Kendall and I occupied. He pulled up a chair and sat between Kendall and me. My legs parted on reflex as he slid his hand between my thighs.

"Who's your friend, Nova?" he asked staring at Kendall.

"Jarvis, this is Kendall, the one that uses my herbs for his tea at his shop," I answered nervously. Kendall held out his hand to shake Jarvis' hand, but he just stared at Kendall's hand until he dropped it.

"Let's go," he said looking at me. Before I could reply Kendall spoke.

Nona Day   Over You

"I promise to make sure she gets home safe. She's having so much fun," Kendall said. "She's going to sing again in a few. Maybe you should stay and listen. She's got a beautiful voice."

I don't even think Jarvis realized how tight he was squeezing my thigh. If I had light skin, I was sure to be bruised tomorrow. I endured the pain, because I would rather he crush my thigh than crush Kendall's face.

"I've heard her best notes," Jarvis said. "I can make her hit a note so high, she'll crack all the windows in here."

"Jarvis please," I said quickly standing up. I normally wouldn't be ashamed of his sexual talk, but I knew he was just being an ass. Jarvis remained seated and leaned forward, staring Kendall down.

"Nova may not see it, but I do, nigga," he said. "Don't fuck with what's mine."

I left him in the lounge. He came out and stood next to me while I waited on the valet. I was furious but I was done draining my energy by arguing with him. The best thing I could do for me and him was save my sanity because his was slowly slipping away. Bahka pulled up in the limo and Jarvis told him to go home. When my car came around, he hopped in the driver's seat and we rode home in complete silence.

Once we arrived at the house, Jarvis took a quick shower and hopped into the bed. Binx hopped on the bed and sat beside him. I knew damn well he wasn't switching sides of me. Then I thought, maybe Binx felt Jarvis needed more protection than I did. After smoking and praying, I moved Binx off the bed and climbed in. For the first time, we slept with our backs to each other.

The Next Morning

I woke up to an empty bed. The potent weed I got from Kendall must've had me sleeping like a baby because I didn't hear Jarvis getting ready for work. Waking up with a serious case of the munchies, I made my way downstairs getting ready to eat the buffet style breakfast Antoine cooked every morning he was here.

"Mr. A not joining you for breakfast this morning?" Antoine asked, placing the prepared dishes on the breakfast table.

"He's here?" I asked.

"I don't know. Is he?" he asked, shrugging his shoulders. "I haven't seen him this morning, so I assumed he was still asleep."

"Don't let anyone clear this table until I say so," I said, standing up. I planned on devouring the food as soon as I found him. I walked toward his study and heard him conducting business over the phone, so I guess he was spending his workday at home. We needed to discuss last night and other things, but I didn't want to do it with anger. *A positive approach is better*, I told myself. I went upstairs and put on the patchwork dress that I wore the night I ruined his evening at the Governor's dinner. I pulled my wild hair back into a ponytail. Grabbing the iPad he had bought me, I made my way to his study. I took a deep breath and walked inside. He looked up and an instant frown appeared on his face.

"Good morning, Mr. Alexandria, my name is Nova Lee Champagne. I'll be your assistant for the day since your permanent one is out sick," I said trying to hold a straight face. Seeing him trying to fight off the curve forming the corners of his mouth made me want to laugh. "Would you care for coffee or tea?"

He sat there staring at me for a few seconds trying not to laugh but eventually he roared with laughter. I stood there as he tried to stop from laughing. Every time he looked at me, he would burst into another uncontrollable laugh. I finally couldn't hold my laughter anymore.

"Stop laughing. You are messing everything up," I said, stomping my feet. After a few minutes, he gained his composure.

"I'm sorry," he said, sitting straight up and trying to have a stern face. "What am I messing up, Nova?" he asked.

"Our role play," I said with a sexy look. He arched a brow. "Now I'm going to go out and reenter. Don't laugh," I demanded.

I left out the room and lightly knocked on the door before entering the study again.

"Hi, I'm Nova Lee Champagne. I'll be your temp assistant for the next six months," I said, walking toward his desk.

"Is that your real name?" he asked with a laugh as he stared at me. I was relieved to see he was willing to play along with me.

"Why? What's wrong with it?" I smiled.

"Your name seems to fit you for some reason."

"What does that mean?" I asked as I started to snoop around in his office as if I'd never been there.

"Your dress seems to match your name," he answered still watching me.

"Do you have a problem with my clothing?" I asked and continued my snooping.

"You dress is blinding. I only allow solids in my place of business," he replied as I made my way to the front of his desk.

"Well I'll remember that the next time I'm called in for a temp job," I said, taking a seat on the edge of his desk.

He stood up, walked to the front of the desk and stood in front of me as I sat on the side of his desk. "You smell like fruit," he said, inhaling my aroma with a hand on my thigh.

"Mr. Alexandria, you're causing my panties to become wet. Or maybe I'm peeing on myself," I said, shamefully dropping my head.

"That pussy juice, Nova Lee," he said staring at me.

"Oh my, I'm so embarrassed," I said. I stared down at the big bulge in his trousers. "Mr. Alexandria, are you sexual aroused?"

"Damn right I am," he said. He reached on the desk and picked up a pair of scissors. "What do you think we should do about it, Nova Lee?" I gasped when he cut my dress open with the scissors and placed them back on the desk. His fingers grazed across my lower lips..

"We can't do this, I'm your employee," I said acting nervous and scared.

"Yes you are. I own you until 4:30. I'm going to taste that sweet smelling pussy and drill my hard dick inside of you as far as it will go," he said, sliding his hand between my thighs and between my petals. I stared at him panting with my mouth gaped slightly open as his fingers stirred my wetness.

Nona Day   Over You

"I want to feel you inside me," I said, opening my legs wider.

"Oh you're going to feel every inch," he said as he stood between my legs. He removed his fingers from me and sucked my juices from them. "Mmmmm, taste even better than you smell." He leaned in and kissed and licked on my neck. I whimpered at the sensation of his tongue caressing me.

I started unbuttoning his shirt. We became so captivated with each other that we became like wild animals. I was trying to tear off his clothes while his mouth stayed connected to my body. I decided I wasn't done playing with him. This was the kind of fun we needed.

"Mr. Alexandria" I murmured, panting for my breath.

"Yes Nova," he uttered as he licked his way down to my center.

"I have to let you know; my petals have never been opened. I'm a virgin," I said. He looked up at me to see me smiling. We both burst into a hysteria of laughter. I stood up and stopped laughing.

Nona Day   Over You

"I'm filing a sexual harassment lawsuit against your company," I said, pushing my way past him. "And you owe me for my dress."

"Not before I get what I want from you first," he said, coming after me as I tried to hurry out of the study laughing. I ran down the hall and out the back door as he chased me in the backyard. We laughed like kids as he chased me around the backyard. I ran back into the house and he chased me around the kitchen and dining room naked. I'm sure his staff thought we had lost our minds, but we had only gotten lost in our own little world. The place I missed being with him so much. He finally cornered me in the living room.

"Oh please, Mr. Alexandria, don't do this to me. I'm just a sweet loving virgin child," I said with pleading eyes.

"When I'm done with you, you will be spoiled and ruined," he said, moving in closer to me.

"Just promise me you won't cum on my dress. It's my favorite. Don't be Bill Clinton. I don't wanna be Monica Lewinsky," I said with sadness, shaking my head. He couldn't hold it any longer. We fell over in laughter. We couldn't stop laughing as we fell on the couch. I stopped laughing, straddled his lap and laid my forehead against his.

"I don't like the place we're at," I said.

"Sorry about last night. You could've told me you didn't want to attend the dinner though," he said.

"You're right and I'm sorry too," I said before kissing his lips softly.

"Nova, that nigga wanna fuck you," he said. Kendall never gave me the impression he was interested in me in that way. Jarvis was greedy when it came to me. He didn't like the thought of sharing me, so I understood why he felt that way.

"He's never tried me like that," I explained. "Even if he did, I belong to you. Do you not know that?"

"Yea, but I don't like a slick ass nigga sniffing around you," he said.

"If he tries anything with me, I'll end the friendship," I said. "I promise."

"Or I'll end him," he said. I didn't doubt for one minute that he would. The sound of the doorbell echoed through the house pulling us from our intimate moment. I tried to get off his lap, but he wrapped his arms around my waist.

"Ain't shit on the other side of that door more important than this," he said. "You ain't happy and we need to figure this shit out."

This is why I loved him. He was crude and distant a lot of times but pulled me back in with love and devotion to me. It was time to have an open and honest talk. The only way to do that was for us to shut out the world and share our deepest thoughts.

I lifted my forehead from his and smiled down at him.

"Can we have a picnic in the backyard tonight and watch Frozen?" I asked.

He laughed. "Yea, we can do that."

Later that Evening

Instead of a picnic, I decided I wanted to get out of the house and have some fun. I used to go bowling with my parents and thought it would be something fun for me and Jarvis to do together. When I walked into his office, he looked frustrated as always when he worked. I took a seat in the chair in front of his desk and started making silly faces, trying to get him to relax and laugh. He looked at me and cracked a smile.

"Did you know if you touch pieces of the same type of metal together in the vacuum of space, they will fuse, bound together until eternity or until you break them apart?" I asked.

"You wanna be metal?" he asked staring at me.

I giggled. "No, I just thought it was interesting. Wouldn't it be awesome to be in a place that fuses us together for eternity?"

"We already in that place," he said. "You ain't going nowhere and I ain't either."

I smiled.

"I wanna go bowling instead of a picnic," I suggested. "And I wanna invite Amoy, Dak, Cache and Noble to come with us.

"Nah, I got some work to do," he said, looking at his computer screen. "But you can go."

I didn't even waste time trying to convince him to come with us. After leaving his office, I went upstairs and got dressed in a pair of high waist, yellow, green, white, and orange pinstripe pants with an orange tee shirt. I strapped my fanny pack across my chest and headed out the door.

We were all at the bowling alley having a blast. Amoy and Cache had no clue how to bowl, but I was giving Dak and Noble some competition.

"I can't believe Jarvis let you come hang with me," Amoy said, as we sat in our bowling section.

"I think he was just happy to get rid of me," I said. "I was distracting him from working."

"Well, you wasn't distracting him too much," Cache said smiling. I followed her eyes to see Jarvis walking over to us. He walked over and kissed me on the cheek, gave Dak and Noble dap, and spoke to Cache. Amoy looked hurt that he didn't even acknowledge her.

"Come on, I'll go with you to get some shoes," I said.

"Ain't putting shoes on my feet that somebody else wore," he said.

Nona Day   Over You

I don't know why he came if he wasn't coming to have fun. His demeanor showed that he didn't want to be here. He wasn't going to ruin my good time. He took a seat as the rest of us continued our game. When it was my turn to bowl, I bent over, wiggled my butt, and looked over my shoulder at Jarvis in an attempt to make him loosen up. He seemed unfazed by my performance. Him being here in his mood was ruining my fun. After bowling a strike, I walked over to him.

"Let's go get a drink," I said.

"Excuse me," a tall, young, black girl walked up to me. "I love your outfit. Especially those pants. Where did you get them?"

I looked at Jarvis and winked my eye. He shook his head and walked away.

"Thank you, I bought them from a thrift shop," I told her.

"Oh dang," she said. "I'll have to see if I can find some similar then."

She smiled at me and walked away. I went inside the bar area of the bowling area to see Jarvis sitting at the bar. I sat beside him.

"See I told you I had style," I said jokingly. All I wanted to do was get him in a better mood.

"They still ugly," he said. I just shook my head.

A young, white guy came and sat at the bar beside us. When the bartender finally walked over, she asked the white guy what he wanted.

"You just gone act like you didn't see me waiting here?" Jarvis asked her angrily. "My damn money spends just like his."

I knew I needed to get him out of here. His mood was dark. If she said the wrong thing to him, I worried how Jarvis would react.

"Sorry, about that," the white bartender said nonchalantly. I had to admit he acted as if he didn't want to serve Jarvis.

"Let's just go home," I said sadly. My fun night was over. Jarvis stood up and smiled at the bartender.

"You own this place?" He asked him.

"No," the bartender replied.

"Good, because I'm buying it the morning and firing yo ass," Jarvis said walking away.

Nona Day   Over You

We went and said goodbye to everyone, before I followed Jarvis home in my car. He went into his office and I went upstairs. My energetic, fun mood was ruined the moment he stepped into the bowling alley. I don't know what time it was when he got into bed and spooned me with kisses on my neck.

"We'll do campfire and a movie tomorrow night," he said. I didn't reply because I had become accustomed to him breaking promises to me.

Jarvis

*M*y presence at the bowling alley ruined her evening. After having my offer declined by two possible investors, I was in a bad mood. Instead of absorbing her positive energy, I fed her my negative vibes. I couldn't ignore it anymore. My entire being felt her drifting away from me. Her love for me was just as strong as mine for her, but she was pulling away from me. She was tired of dealing with my unstable emotions. Hell, I was tired of dealing with them. It was time to fix me, so I could save us. She had done everything she could to keep me sane. She needed my help in making that happen. At a time murder and mayhem helped me cope with my emotions. After killing those involved in Brandon's death, my conflicted emotions were still running rapid inside of me.

I was in my man cave when Rochelle walked in.

"Sorry to interrupt, sir, but Ms. Valentine is at the door," she said. "She's pretty adamant about speaking with you.

"Show her to my office," I said. I smoked a blunt and let Valentine wait for me. She knew I didn't like unannounced visits at my home.

When I entered my home office, Valentine was pacing the floor. She stopped and glared at me through murderous eyes. I knew she was pissed because I kept her waiting but that wasn't my concern. She sat in the chair in front of my desk while I sat behind it.

"You are so obnoxious," she said staring at me. I chuckled and shrugged my shoulders. I wasn't going to argue with her truth.

"Why are you at my home without an invite?" I asked, leaning back in the chair.

"I'm starting to regret trying to help your ass," she said.

"How exactly are you here to help me, Valentine?"

There was no bitterness between us since I ruined her wedding day. Valentine was too ambitious to let her heart interfere with making money. We'd invested in a few projects together that had put a nice savings in her account. I'd also considered letting her lead the bank's legal team. I needed someone who would have my best interest and I knew she would be the perfect choice.

"I know you're caught up in this newfound love thing, but you need to pull your head out the clouds," she warned me. "You're on the verge of being cut out of something you've started."

"And what is that?" I asked.

"I've been having pillow talk with Marvin," she said. "Him and a few of your investors are considering shutting you out of the bank you're trying to build. They think your behavior lately is a threat to their careers."

There was that reckless anger that started to build inside me again. The anger that made me do impulsive shit without thinking of the repercussions. I would kill every last one of them before I let them shut me out of something I started. I kept my composure in front of Valentine because she didn't know the other side of me, but my body was starting to heat up like a furnace.

"Who's in on this move?" I asked, ready to handle each of them. She called out the names.

"They're meeting at AG in the Ritz Carlton tonight at eight," she said.

"Why you telling me this?" I asked.

"You are a business minded beast. All four of them together could never accomplish what you can," she said, standing up. "Now, don't make me regret choosing the wrong side because I'll be back to collect my favor one day."

Watching her walk out of the office reminded me what I found sexy about her, but she wasn't Nova. No one was Nova. Every time I tried to do right and make time for us something got in my way. We needed time for each other, but I couldn't be lounging on a damn beach while they took my goal from me. I couldn't disappoint my father that way.

A few minutes later, I made my way toward the kitchen. All I could hear was laughter. She had brought so much life to this house. When I walked into the kitchen, the entire staff was sitting around while Nova and Antoine cooked.

"Now, y'all gotta be honest," Nova said. "Don't be choosing Antoine just because he's the chef."

"So, they should choose you because you keep the boss' bed warm?" Antoine asked jokingly.

"Yep," Nova replied. Everyone laughed. She looked up and saw me standing at the kitchen entrance. Everyone looked at me and immediately stood up. I was a stern boss and kept a professional relationship with them. Well, everyone except Bahka.

"Y'all sit down," Nova said, walking toward me. They looked at me and I nodded my head for them to have a seat. "We're having a taste off. Me and Antoine are making appetizers for our movie night. You can be the tie breaker since they're six tasters."

I had to break her heart right now. Movie night had to be canceled because I needed to end this takeover shit Marvin had cooked up. She looked so excited and here I was getting ready to ruin that happiness. It seemed that was all I was good at doing, ruining shit for the people I loved. She didn't deserve this from me.

"Nova, I need to talk to you," I said. She looked up at me and I could see the cheerful life draining from her eyes. I didn't have to tell her our plans were canceled, because she felt it. Her smile slowly left her face. Without saying a word, she walked out of the kitchen. For some reason my eyes landed on Bahka. He just shook his head.

Nona Day   Over You

There was no point in trying to explain this situation to Nova, because I was wrong. She didn't look at my life the way I did, so she would never understand. Instead of going upstairs to stare into her sad eyes, I left the house and went to my condo.

Later That Evening

When I showed up at the meeting where Marvin, Carl, and Charlotte and Priscilla's husbands, they were shocked. These were grimy men that moved like snakes. It sucked the life out of me to sit there calmly negotiating with them. By the time the meeting ended, I felt it in my gut that they still had plans of shutting me out. I had to make moves before it happened.

After the meeting, I was sitting at a table at AG having a drink at the bar. I kept trying to call Nova. Her phone kept going straight to voicemail. She had every right to be furious with me. I had let her down time and time again. Here I was trying to be the nigga everybody wanted me to be and still mothafuckas went against me. All she ever wanted from me was to love her the way she deserved. I was hurting the one person that I knew without a doubt loved the good and bad in me.

Nona Day   Over You

It was time to go home and deal with the disappointed look in Nova's face as well as my own shit. I sat in the back of the limo as Bahka drove. When he stopped at a stop light, a little voice inside me told me to look to my left. A fire that had been building inside of me for some time now went up in flames. I knew I was getting ready to lose it, but I couldn't stop. So much shit had been building up inside me for too long. Seeing that nigga wrap his arms around her sent me over the edge. They were standing in front of the neo-soul lounge she attended with him once before. Maybe it was more than one time. The biggest smile was on her face. It made me think of the sadness that I caused her. This nigga was giving her the happiness that she wanted.

Before I knew it, I was out of the limo and my feet led me toward them. I could hear Bahka calling my name, but my focus was on Nova and her friend. The shock and fear in her eyes didn't deter me from stomping her date to the ground. I couldn't remember the first or last fist I rammed into his face. I couldn't remember anything until I was held down by Bahka and a couple of other dudes. I couldn't see her, but I could hear Nova's cries. I could hear people yelling to call the ambulance and the police, but I couldn't see anyone. Bahka's big ass body was blocking my view from seeing her.

"Come on!" Bahka said, pulling me off the ground by my collar. "We gotta get da fuck outta here!"

"Get Nova!" I barked at him trying to see her. I spotted her kneeling down by her friend trying to help him. He was still alive, but I could see the blood on his face. Bahka hauled me to the car and threw me in the backseat.

I beat a man in front of witnesses and had finally destroyed my life.

*****

Bahka wanted me to get out of Atlanta ASAP, but there was no point in running. I was sure there were numerous cameras filming me beating the guy. I couldn't even remember his name, but he was the victim of all the shit I was feeling inside. After Bahka dropped me off, I sent him to check on the guy's condition and Nova. I sat in my pitch-black house waiting for the cops to show up.

Nona Day   Over You

They hadn't come before I drunk myself to sleep with Binx sitting on the bed with me.

I was awakened by Nova walking into the bedroom. She didn't even look at me as she made her way to the bathroom. The energy I felt from her sent chills down my spine. Sitting up on side of the bed, I heard the shower come on. When she came out, I didn't know what to say to her. She was so calm, and her face showed no anger. I watched her as she dropped the towel that was wrapped around her and started to get dress. She put on the same clothes she wore the night I brought her here.

I could feel my chest tightening, because I knew this was the end of us. She was leaving me, and there wasn't anything I could do to stop her this time. After she was dressed, she turned to face me.

"I'm sure you don't give a damn, but Kendall is going to be fine," she said with water in her eyes. A huge weight left my shoulders. The guy didn't deserve what I had done to him.

I walked over to her as she stood in front of the dresser and reached for her. She needed to know how sorry and bad I felt for what I had done.

Nona Day   Over You

"Don't touch me!" She screamed at me, knocking my arm away.

"Nova, I wouldn't hurt you," I said.

"I know that, but I don't want to hear your sorries," she said as her eyes started to tear up. "I poured so much of myself into you trying to love you in a way that would heal and support you. I have given everything I have to you; I have nothing left, not anything for myself."

Tears flowed uncontrollably from her eyes. All I wanted to do was hold her and try to give her back everything she'd given me, but it was too late.

"Do you know how much this hurts me to walk away from you?" she asked looking up at me. "Every fiber in my body is consumed by you. I don't know who I am without you anymore. My life feels completely empty now because I gave it to you."

The anguish in her eyes, tremble in her voice and defeat in her body was killing me on the inside. I caused this by pulling her back into my life. My heart wouldn't let my eyes see her walk out of my life forever, so they closed before I saw her walk out of the bedroom.

Days Later

"Jarvis!" I heard Amoy calling my name repeatedly.

I was in a miserable drunken fog and didn't know how many days had passed since Nova left. All I could remember of Nova was the depleted look on her face. I'd spent my time guzzling down bottles of liquor to try and ruin my life. The pain of losing her was unbearable. I brought her back into my life and she gave me all of her.. Losing her wasn't what hurt me the most. It was the fact that I disappointed her by not being the man she deserved. I picked up the bottle of Cognac sitting on the floor beside me and chugged it down until the bottle was empty. Every time I felt myself sobering up, I used liquor and weed to numb the pain in my chest and the sickness in my gut.

The opening of the greenhouse door caused the bright sunlight to shine through and I immediately rubbed my eyes. The night Nova left I came to her greenhouse just to be around something she loved. Amoy stood in the doorway staring at me.

"Oh Jarvis," she said sadly, walking over to me and bending down on her knees in front of me. I looked up to see her eyes full of tears.

"I fucked up Amoy," I mumbled. "I'm sorry. I tried to do right by her."

"I know you did," she said, wrapping her arms around me. I cried when my parents died. I shed tears for the love I had for Nova and the hurt I caused her, but the cry for help that I let out as Amoy consoled me was agonizing pain. My baby sister held my overgrown broken ass until I stopped crying. "Come on, let's go in the house."

I staggered inside the sliding kitchen door with her help. There was no way she could help me upstairs, so I stumbled to one of the bedrooms on the bottom floor. Lying on my back the room started to spin, so I quickly turned on my stomach.

I woke up with a pounding headache wondering how I made it to the bedroom. The alcohol had diminished the pain I was feeling but being sober brought it all back. I went to the bathroom and pissed a bladder full of liquor. After taking a hot shower, I put on a T-shirt and jeans. The alcohol had made me forget the time and day, so I searched for my phone to find out. My heart jumped when I saw it on the nightstand plugged up. *She's back!* I rushed downstairs.

The disappointment of seeing Amoy sitting in the den scrolling through her phone shattered my heart all over again. I loved my sister, but she wasn't the one I wanted to see.

"Come in the kitchen," she said, standing up. "I'll make you some coffee."

I sat at the kitchen table silently while she made coffee. The house was so quiet; it felt empty without her energy filling it with joy. I wondered what she was doing at this very moment and if she was alright.

Amoy sat the coffee in front of me and took a seat across from me.

"You hungry?" she asked.

"Have you talked to her?" My empty stomach wasn't my concern. I wasn't going to bother her, but I needed to know how she was doing.

"She's hurting like you, but she's going to be okay just like you," she said. "She just needs to focus on herself."

"What day is it?" I asked.

She half smiled. "Thursday. You've been MIA for four days. I wanted to give you some time to yourself, but I was worried about you. Do you remember Dak dragging yo drunk ass out the club?"

I didn't remember going to Dak's club, let alone being dragged out.

"Nah," I said.

"Yea, you was there showing yo ass," she said, shaking her head. "He had to pull you out because you was beefing with some niggas about stealing a bottle from your table."

All I could do was shake my head.

Reality hit me that the cops hadn't come to arrest me yet. There was no way the incident hadn't gone viral yet.

"Have the cops been looking for me?" I asked.

"No, Kendall didn't file charges," she said. "You probably can thank Nova for that."

I dropped my head thinking of the state of rage I was in. That trapped anger burst out of me like a mad man and I unleashed it on someone that didn't deserve it.

"I need to apologize and pay whatever medical bills he has," I said.

"You'll pay me back for his medical bills," she said. "You can apologize once you get yourself together."

Her eyes were full of pity for me.

"Where is everybody?" I asked, referring to my staff.

"I gave them all a few days off. It's sibling time," she said smiling at me.

"You ain't gotta do that shit, Amoy," I said. "I know I'm the last nigga you wanna be around."

She stared at me and her eyes instantly welled up with tears.

"Jarvis, I love you and will always be here for you. I know I'm overbearing and judgmental sometimes. That's only because I want the best for you. There's nothing on this earth that you can do that would make me turn away from you."

I leaned back and sat up straight in the chair.

"Aunt Belle?" I asked, remembering the look on her face when she found out I killed her.

She reached over and placed her hand on top of mine.

Nona Day   Over You

"I was angry because of the secrets that were kept from me. I never blamed you for what you did because I understood that feeling of betrayal and hurt that she caused us," she said. "Nova explained so much to me about what you've been feeling, and I'm so sorry for not letting you know how much you mean to me. I don't want you to be anyone but yourself. I love and support you, not some-damn-body you're pretending to be. And fuck those people that don't want the loyal and protective Jarvis I know and love."

The sincerity in her eyes meant everything to me. All I ever wanted was to know she loved and accepted me regardless.

"You know if I could dig her up and kill her again, I would," I said honestly.

"And I would be there to help you dig her up," she said seriously.

I dropped my head a few seconds before looking up at her.

"The week of Ma and Pop's deaths I was on punishment. You know how stubborn and hardheaded I was," I said. She laughed and nodded her head. "I was so mad at him because I couldn't attend Axel's big birthday party because I was on punishment. Every night he came into the bedroom to say goodnight, and he would tell me he loved me. I never said it back. For four days, I never told him I loved him, Amoy. He died not hearing me say those three damn words that meant so much to him."

She held my hand and squeezed it.

"Jarvis, you didn't have to tell Daddy you loved him because he knew that. He would be so damn proud of who you are today. The way you took care of me when you didn't have to shows you're just as amazing as he was. I can see him gently slapping you on the back of your head and saying…that's the shit I'm talking about son."

I laughed because he always did that when I did something to make him proud.

"Guess I need to get my shit together once again," I said.

"Yea, but no doing it on your own this time. You got me," she said.

A Few Days Later

Nova

*T*he past ten days had been the hardest struggle of my life. I felt empty, broken and drained. The pain of walking away from him was still buried deep in my heart. My life was so consumed with him; I felt lost without him. Pulling myself out of bed was a chore, and prayer and meditation were distant memories. All I could do was cry and try to sleep the hurt away. Every day I woke up hoping the pain would be easier to bear or magical disappear. It seemed to get worse and I didn't have the strength to heal myself. I hadn't even picked up the phone to call Kendall. The guilt I felt for causing his assault was too much.

The knock on my she shed door irritated me. I knew it was only Ma or Daddy coming to check on me. Every breakfast, lunch and dinner, one of them would bring me a plate. I looked on my small nightstand to see it was lunch time. I drug my heavy, but empty, body out of the bed to unlock the door. When I opened the door, my heart plummeted to my feet. Never in a million years did I think he would come here, but here he stood holding Binx. I was so stunned; I wanted to slam the door in his face and crawl under the bed, but my body wouldn't move. He couldn't do this to me. I wasn't strong enough to turn him away.

"Can we talk?" he asked. My heart knew how much I missed him. But the sound of his voice made my body ache for him.

My tongue felt too heavy to speak, so I shook my head. He couldn't be here. I wanted to plead with him to leave me be, but I couldn't speak. Tears started to fill up my eyes.

"I just…," he spoke before I finally found the strength to say something.

"No!" I blurted out, quickly wiping the stubborn tears.

"I just wanted to bring you Binx," he said, putting Binx down. Binx rubbed against my leg and purred.

He stood there staring at me, giving me the strength that my body needed desperately. His eyes pulled me into his soul, and I started to feel revived. I could feel his energy flowing through my body as it heated up. My heart stared beating against my chest when he stepped closer to me. It felt like a hopeless battle to find the hold he had on me, but

I dug deep inside myself. I found an inkling of power to deny him.

"Nova." He said my name with a soft, loving yearning; it caused a shiver down my spine.

I find the courage to take a few steps back.

"You gotta leave," I said, turning to walk away. The only place I could escape to was my small bathroom. Before I could get away from him, he gently grabbed my arm. Tingling shock waves spread through my body. More tears poured from my eyes as I fought to hold on to me.

"Nova please," he said, turning me around to face me. "I fucked up, but I'm trying to fix shit."

He looked so sad, desperate and needy. Something clicked inside of me. I helped do this to him, myself and us. Jarvis pulled me back into his life, because he needed me. I could've walked away but I wanted his love, so I happily became his crutch.

"I'm guilty of loving you too much. I was so scared of you getting over me, I abused your need for me. As long as you needed me, I had a place in your life. That's just how desperate I was to have your love," I told him. "But I lost myself trying to keep it."

"I did shit all wrong, Nova," he said. "Just gimme a chance to make it right between us."

I wanted to make things right between us more than anything, but I had to make things right within myself. There was no way I could do that trying to be his sanity. We needed time apart to find ourselves again. We were beautiful together but lost apart.

"Oh, didn't know you had company," Daddy said, walking inside. "You okay?"

Daddy may've admired and respected Jarvis, but I was still his baby girl. He knew how hurt I was over our breakup, so he was being a protective dad. He walked over to me, stood beside me and stared at Jarvis. If I wasn't so distraught right now, this would've been funny. Daddy stood tall like he had any chance of beating Jarvis.

"She's good, Mr. Champagne," Jarvis said. "I was just bringing her Binx."

"Well, why don't you let me walk you out," Daddy said, walking toward the door. He stood at the door waiting on Jarvis while Jarvis stayed staring at me. His eyes told me this wouldn't be the last time I saw him. He turned and walked out the door with Daddy. Just as quick as he came and revived me, watching him walking away broke my heart. I flopped down on my bed not knowing how to get through this alone. All my parents told me to do was pray to God to heal my pain. They didn't understand my God was inside me. Me, who was lost. In order to pray for healing, I needed to manifest into my highest self. A place where I felt happy and whole on the inside. I needed a complete a spiritual cleansing.

The Next Day

For the first time in over a week, I left my she shed. I woke up this morning, prayed, meditated, did yoga and started my journey back to myself. My parents were happy when I showed up for breakfast. Ma let me use her car, because I didn't have the car Jarvis bought me anymore. My first stop was to see Kendall. I was happy to see the bruises on his face were healing nicely.

"I'm so sorry it took me so long to come see you," I said, sitting on his sofa.

"It's cool, Nova," he said. "I know things were probably rough for you too. How you been doing?"

"Horrible, but I'm trying to get it together," I said honestly. He nodded his head.

There was an awkward silence between us. I wanted to apologize for what Jarvis did, but I wasn't going to make this visit about Jarvis. Everything from this point on was about restoring me.

"You back together?" he asked. I shook my head but was curious as to why he asked me. We never discussed my relationship, because our friendship wasn't on that level. Maybe he had the right to know since he was attacked because of my relationship. "You know I didn't press charges?"

It surprised me that he didn't have Jarvis locked up. I hadn't turned on my phone, laptop or looked at television in over a week, but I assumed Jarvis had been charged with some kind of assault charge. It was a relief to know that Kendall didn't press charges.

"Why?" I asked.

"He was right, Nova," he said looking at me. "I had feelings for you."

"Kendall," I said, trying to find the words to say to him. He never gave me the impression that he liked me, or maybe I was so in love with Jarvis that I never saw it. Regardless, I didn't see Kendall that way. He was fun to be around and had become my escape from the life that was draining me.

"You don't have to say anything," he said. "When he showed up at the lounge, I knew I stood no chance. It was obvious how much you loved him."

"I'm sorry if I gave you mixed signals," I said.

He chuckled. "You didn't. Your soothing energy is just magnetic."

I forced a smile. "Well, I'm trying to find the energy again. It seems I lost it along with everything else inside me."

"I hope this doesn't mean we can't be friends. Trust me, I would never try you. It's detrimental to my well-being," he said jokingly.

"Yea, we can still hang sometimes," I said smiling at him.

*****

Nona Day   Over You

After leaving Kendall's apartment, I made a trip to my spiritual advisor and to the store to pick up some candles, sage and oils. It was time to get back to the goofy, fun Nova Lee. I didn't know if that was possible after experiencing and losing a love so deep, but I was going to try. My last stop was lunch with Amoy and Cache at Noble's place.

"We're so glad you came," Cache said, hugging me tight.

"We missed you," Amoy said with a warm hug. We took a seat at the table.

"I'm sorry for going MIA," I said.

The night I left Jarvis, I called Amoy to let her know I had left and why. I didn't need her to be there for me, but I knew Jarvis needed her. After I hung up with her that night, I turned off my phone. When I turned it back on this morning, I had several text messages from her and Cache.

"That's okay," Amoy said. "We're just happy to see you."

"Thanks," I said. "I'm not going to stay long. I just wanted to see y'all. I miss the wine and weed dates."

Nona Day   Over You

They giggled.

"You ain't gotta rush off," Cache said. "Jarvis is out of town."

Amoy nudged her arm, making me laugh.

"It's okay to say his name," I said. "I can't heal and restore myself by ignoring the biggest part of losing myself. He came to see me."

"He did?" Amoy asked surprised.

"Yea, it was kinda intense," I said. "I blamed him for a lot of things I was responsible for myself. I just can't go back to the way things were."

"We understand," Cache said. "You can't love him and lose yourself."

"Are you going back to Dothan?" Amoy asked.

"No. Right now, I'm isolating myself for a while, so please don't take it personally. When I'm ready, I'll hit you guys up," I said.

"Take all the time you need. We'll be here to smoke and drink when you ready," Cache said smiling.

Nova

*M*editation, yoga, praying and manifesting was all I did until I felt like the old me. After a couple more weeks of finding the strength to pull myself together, I spent the next two weeks in Brazil since I had enough money saved. Time alone with the universe was what I needed to fully restore myself. The blessing in knowing myself again allowed me to elevate from a negative place inside me. It was time to let the past go.

The night I walked out of Jarvis' life to save my own felt like I left a part of me. I was trying to hold on to a love that was becoming more powerful than being true to myself. He still was deep in my heart and I knew he would always be. I'd learned to accept that and still love him, but I couldn't love him without loving myself. He crossed my mind every day; I wondered how he was doing and did he miss me anymore. Even though I still loved him with all my heart, I had made peace with not having him in my life. The time I spent reflecting on my life helped me find a purpose. The excitement of starting a new adventure had me hyped.

"Nova, you wanna ride to the mall with me?" Ma asked. I was lounging on the sofa reading *The Secret.* I'd read it numerous times before, and it was one of my favorites.

"I'm good, Ma," I said. "Can you bring me back some licorice?" I seldom went to the mall. If I did, I was in and out. I knew going with Ma would be an all-day adventure.

She laughed. "Girl, get yo behind up and come with me."

I sighed. I hadn't been off the farm since I returned from Brazil two months ago, so I guess it was time to get back into the real world.

"Nova Lee Champagne, get up. I need a new dress for the pastor's anniversary and your father needs some shoes."

"Ma, you not supposed to buy a man shoes," I reminded her. "They'll walk out of your life with them on their feet."

"Chile, yo daddy won't get far with the cheap shoes I buy," she said jokingly. I laughed.

Nona Day   Over You

"You gon' let me pick out a dress for you?" I teased. She hated my style as much as Jarvis. Just thinking about him still held a hole in my heart that couldn't be healed. No matter how much I prayed that empty feeling was still there. For a while, I wanted him to come take away the void I was feeling. Other times, I was thankful he loved me enough to stay away.

"Yea chile, you're more than welcome to pick out my dress," she said smiling down at me. "When I'm dead."

The laughter that came from me was rare and necessary. I pulled myself off the couch and got dressed. With my red, brown, beige, white, purple, yellow, dark green, long, peasant skirt, ivory lace top and cork heeled sandals I was ready. We hopped in her Camry and made our way to the mall. Ma kept glancing at me as she drove. I had been so thankful for having her shoulder to cry on. Plus, my spiritual advisor had helped me tremendously in getting back to a place where I felt like myself.

"Why you keep looking at me?" I asked her.

"I finally see the old Nova," she said, smiling at me. I could tell she wanted to say more, so I gave her the opportunity.

"But," I said, encouraging her to speak her mind.

"There's a sadness in your eyes," she said. "Have you thought about reaching out to him?"

"No Ma, and I don't plan on it," I stated firmly. "Please don't bring him up. It still hurts."

She reached over and massaged my shoulder.

"I know, baby girl," she said. "It's gonna take a lot of time to get over a once in a lifetime kind of love."

I knew I'd never get over him. Having the strength to endure every day without him was my forever goal.

*****

Ma dragged me to just about every store in the mall. I was worn out while she still was in shopaholic mode, so I decided to get us a smoothie while she shopped. As I walked past Victoria's Secret, I realized I hadn't shaved any part of my body in the last three months. My only focus had been my inner self. The last thing I worried about was hair growing where I didn't want it. I let out a deep sigh when I approached the smoothie shop because of the long line.

"What's your name, beautiful?" asked the tall young man standing behind me. I looked over my shoulder at him. He was definitely handsome in a rugged kind of way. He reminded me of that football player Michael Vick.

"Nova," I said with a smile. "Anybody ever told you, you resemble Michael Vick?"

"I get that a lot. I'm Dirk. It's nice to meet you," he said with a charming grin. While the line moved slowly, Dirk flirted. He was definitely a charmer. I finally made it to the counter and placed my order. After I received my order, I stepped out the way.

"I would love to have your number, so I can get to know you better," he said before I walked away.

"I'm sorry. This is just a very bad time for me," I said as I turned and walked away.

I slowly made my way back to the store. I was window shopping as I strolled through the crowded mall. I looked ahead and nearly dropped both my smoothies. My feet turned into blocks of cement. My heart started to race as adrenaline pumped rapidly through my veins. He was there dressed in light blue jeans, a Polo style shirt and Dolce and Gabbana sneakers, holding Valentine's hand. He laughed as she leaned in and hugged him. He generously returned her embrace. Seeing him happily enjoying her company broke my heart. I crashed into Dirk spilling my smoothies all over the front of his clothing. I heard laughter around me. I was so embarrassed. I couldn't believe this was happening to me right now.

"I'm so sorry," I said as I stepped back looking at the green smoothies smeared over Dirk's clothing.

"Now you *have* to give me your phone number," he said with a sexy smile as he looked at me.

He didn't understand how sick to my stomach I was at that moment. It took everything in me not to add my vomit to the green smoothies on his clothes. I quickly called out my phone number and rushed past him and out of the mall. It wasn't my problem if he didn't get it. It wasn't like I was going to go out with him anyway. I literally wanted to crawl under a rock and die. Once I was outside of the mall, I burst into tears trying to hold back the panic attack that was building up inside me. After calming myself down, I called Ma, because I was ready to get as far away from the mall as possible. Maybe it was time for me to get back to my simple life in Dothan.

The drive back to the house was quiet. Daddy knew something was wrong with me the moment I stepped in the house.

"What's wrong with you?" Daddy asked. I ignored his question and sat Ma's bags on the center table.

"Poor baby just still heart broken," Ma answered for me.

When we got back to my parents' house, Daddy took us out for dinner. They were excited to hear about my new project. I had a lot of work to do if I wanted to make this happened. This was a project with a purpose. After we got home, I went to my she shed and started my research.

Two Days Later

I didn't let seeing Jarvis with Valentine crush my spirit. Accepting what was and what is was a part of my healing process. He was moving on with his life and it was time I did the same. Dirk had called me the same night I gave him my phone number. He had just move to Atlanta from Detroit. There was no way I was looking to get

Nona Day   Over You

involved with anyone, but it was time to move on. I decided to go to a house party with him. He promised it was a nice, mature gathering so I took his word.

I was in complete shock when I walked into the house; the sight almost knocked me off my feet. There stood Bahka opening the door for us. When Bahka laid eyes on me, he nearly crushed me wrapping his big, husky arms around me. A double whammy was finding out Dirk was Bahka's nephew. Once we were inside, Bahka introduced me to everyone. Shortly after, I saw him having a heated conversation with Dirk. There wasn't a doubt in my mind that talk was about Jarvis and me. A few minutes later, Dirk came over; I was getting acquainted with Bahka's wife, Lisah. She was really nice and helped me relax in a house full of strangers.

"You drinking?" Dirk asked.

"I'll take a vodka and cranberry," I said. My rule was a one drink minimum tonight. It didn't matter that Bahka was there. He wasn't my protector any more than Jarvis was. I needed to keep a level head.

It wasn't long before I was having a good time. Dirk was charming, funny and attentive. He made sure not to forget I was there with him, but I was enjoying mingling with everyone without him. A familiar voice made me nervous. As I stood by the dining room entrance talking to a woman named Shirley, I turned around to see Axel. My heart started to pound wondering would Jarvis be arriving. There was an eerie feeling in my gut that told me that he would be. Feeling flushed, I walked out the sliding doors that led to an outdoor pool. I took a deep breath of fresh air to try and relax. I gave myself a pep talk. Even if he was here, I held the divine power within myself to handle seeing him again.

I don't know how long I had been standing outside meditating peacefully while a party was going on inside. My body, mind and soul had zoned out. I was so relaxed I didn't feel or smell his presence standing behind me until I turned around and ruined his light blue shirt with my vodka and cranberry drink.

"Clumsy ass," he said smiling at me. *That smile.* My God how much I'd missed it. I hadn't seen those pearly whites in so long. He looked peaceful, relaxed and happy. There was a different aura about him.

"I-I'm so sorry," I said anxiously, but I decided to not make this moment awkward. "You shouldn't sneak up on people, stalker."

Nona Day   Over You

That laugh! His simple laughter sent chills through me. He looked at me still smiling. And just like that time stopped as our eyes met. We went to a place only we shared together. That place was still there, intact and untouched. Nothing had changed, except the light in his eyes.

"Nova," he said my name. This time it wasn't filled with desperation. It flowed with love and peace. "How you been?"

Don't make this hard, Nova. He's just trying to be cordial. No reason to make this complicated. Relax, breathe and release. I spoke those words in my head before replying.

"You know, just kicking it and hanging high, low and loose," I said humorously.

He laughed. "You so damn goofy."

I giggled.

"Nova, we bout to play charades," Dirk said, poking his head out of the sliding door. Jarvis looked over his shoulder at Dirk, and I stopped breathing for a brief moment. All I remembered was him beating Kendall. Dirk stepped out on the patio as if he was staking his claim.

Jarvis looked back at me. For a brief second, I thought he was going to drag my behind from the party, but he stepped to the side to let me walk past him. My stubborn feet wouldn't move from his presence. Shirley walked out on the patio interrupting the quiet tension.

"Y'all come on," she said. "We picking names for partners."

I finally found movement in my feet but felt his pull as I walked away.

Jarvis

$\mathcal{I}$ never thought I would run into her at Bahka's spot. The moment I stepped through the door, he informed me that she was there with his cousin. I can't lie and say it didn't piss me off, because it did. Showing my ass wasn't going to get me back to where I wanted to be with her, so I decided to try and play it cool. When I walked out on the patio, I chuckled at her outlandish outfit, but seeing her from behind in uncoordinated, multicolored clothes was absolutely beautiful. I'd seen Nova meditate enough to know she was in her own little world, so I decided not to interrupt her. My heart led my feet to stay close behind her; her clumsy ass turned around and ruined my shirt. She was the old Nova…weird, goofy and funny.

I stood outside a few minutes just reflecting on how much I missed her. There wasn't anything I didn't miss about her. The big ass house was quiet again. My bedroom was too neat and organized. Even the staff moped around missing her, but never asked me about her whereabouts. Hell, I even missed Binx's mean mugging ass. We had developed a bond after she left. I was getting ready to step back inside when Axel stepped outside.

"You good?" He asked.

"Yea," I replied. He walked up to me. We were the same height, so we were staring straight into each other's eyes.

"I know you nigga. Been in the sandboxes with you," he said. "Don't do stupid shit. If you want the nigga out the way, I got you. Ain't no charge for it either."

"You got beef with the nigga or something?" I asked.

Axel chuckled. "Nah, I just know that shit bothers you to see her with someone else. If it bothers you, it bothers me."

That was the kind of bond Axel and I had. We handled shit for each other.

Dirk stepped out on the patio.

"I'm good. He ain't a problem," I assured Axel. Axel walked back inside.

Dirk walked over to me. I knew this nigga wasn't going to try to come at me about Nova. I said a quick prayer asking God to please not let him do that. He stood facing me, but I stood a few inches taller than him.

"Nova's here with me tonight," he said.

"You got it but sounds like you trying to convince yourself more than me," I said smiling at him. I walked back into the house, stood by the bar and cleaned my shirt with a few napkins. Dirk walked over to Nova and put his arm around Nova's waist. She nicely slid her slender frame out his arm. *That's my baby.*

"Half the people's names are in the bag; I will let the ones whose name isn't in the bag pull. Whoever's name you get, that's your partner," Lisha, Bahka's wife, said. I kept my head down scrolling through my phone.

"Seems like you're my partner, stalker boy," I heard her angelic voice. "I don't play to lose, so you better get it right."

"Man, shut da fuck up," I said laughing as I stood up. This was the old us before things got complicated. This was the best of us.

She smiled. She started to reach out for my hand, but instantly changed her mind. She waved for me to follow her to where everyone was crowded to begin the game.

We sat side by side on a sofa with another couple. On reflex my hand almost went between her thighs.

"Uh-uh, can't touch this…hammer time," she said. I laughed hysterically. She was so damn goofy and beautiful. I realized how much I had held the person that I enjoyed the most from being herself. This was the Nova that knew how to make me laugh and be happy without force. I had forced her to bring me happiness when we were together. That drained her. It was so hard not to touch her, to feel her soft silky skin. I inhaled to breathe in her sweet aroma that I was still addicted to. Even though we made sure not to touch each other we had fun together. We laughed and talked together like best friends.

"Nova, you bout ready?" Dirk said looking at her. The games had ended but everyone was still laughing and talking.

"Yea, I'm ready," she said as she stood from the sofa. Nova turned to face me. "Good game," she said with a smile. We had won the game of charades. I nodded my head at her. I was pissed that she was leaving with him. She should've been going home with me. Sex wasn't even the reason I wanted to take her home with me. I just wanted to be in her presence and enjoy her company alone. Just me and her.

An hour later, everyone started to leave.

"Jar, I don't know why you let her leave with Dirk. You know you still love that girl," Lisah said to me as I stood up to leave.

"Mind yo damn business," Bahka yelled at her as she walked away.

"I wanna know how da hell yo wife know my business," I said to Bahka.

"Pillow talk, mothafucka," he said before blowing out smoke from the cigar. "Something you ain't getting tonight."

"Big pussy whipped nigga," I said, walking toward the front door.

"At least I wasn't crying and throwing up," he yelled. "Lovesick ass nigga."

I had to laugh as I walked out the house.

The Next Day

Nona Day   Over You

I called a meeting for the four black men that were initially going to invest with me. Marvin, Carl, Charlotte and Priscilla's husbands, Terrence and Richard. A few white investors sat at the big conference table in my office at Galaxy Enterprise.

"I want to thank each of you for coming here today before I say what I need to say," I said.

"Jarvis, there's no need for the meeting," Marvin said. "We've all made our decision to not invest in your banking institution."

"I'm not even sure why we're here," Paul said.

"Oh, I know you're not investing," I said. "I also know the group of men seated at this table are investing in opening a bank together."

I stood up and walked around the table placing a manila envelope in front of all of them.

"In those envelopes is each of your true characters," I said as I placed the envelopes. "From the day you all welcomed a nigga like me into your entitled circle, you have judged me, and I allowed you to disrespect me and my people in ways that should've costed each one of you your lives."

"What's in here?" Carl asked picking up the envelope.

"Don't open it yet," I ordered. "You and the other black men sitting at this table are the worse kind of black men I've ever dealt with. You think because you have a little money and power that privileged, entitled mothafuckas like Paul, Chad and Randall give a fuck about you. We just token niggas that allows them to think they aren't racist."

"Jarvis, I know you're upset about not getting investors, but this isn't the way to handle it," Paul said. "Men of our power can ruin you without lifting a finger."

I sat back down in my seat. "And a nigga like me ain't to be fucked with. Now, you may open your gifts."

I had enough dirt on each one of them to bury their careers for good. The white men faces turned whiter. The black men looked like they had seen a ghost they were so scared. Terrence jumped from his seat in a fit of rage.

"You've been fucking my wife?" He asked furiously.

I chuckled. "Nah, she was fucking me. Your concern should be the information of you helping her brother hide his drug money and help finance his many meth labs."

"How much do you want?" Chad asked.

"I don't want your money," I said. "The bank idea will be dismantled and whatever investments any of us have together will end as of today. I'll even be nice and pay back whatever you invested."

"You can't do this," Carl said. "We know you run a drug cartel."

I leaned back in my seat and lit a blunt. "Prove it nigga."

The business meeting ended with each man reluctantly agreeing to bow out keeping the squeaky clean images intact. Now, it was time to put my energy into getting back with one thing I couldn't live without…her love.

She ignored all my calls and texts, so I showed up knocking on her door. I knew she was inside, because I stopped at her parents' house before coming to her little ass shed. After being ignored, I turned the doorknob and was happy it opened the door. She was sitting in her small meditation area with her eyes closed. That explained why she ignored my knocks. I walked over and sat across from her. She slowly opened her eyes.

Nona Day   Over You

"I wanna know how to love you," I said staring at her. Her face remained calm, but our bodies were so in sync I felt the rush she was feeling from being so close to me.

"Jarvis, you'll never know until you learn to forgive and love yourself," she said. She stood up and I followed her out the shed. "I can't do this again."

I gently grabbed her arm to stop her from walking away from me.

"I'm not here to get over you this time. I don't need you to love me because I don't know how to love myself. I'm here because I wanna love yo nappy headed ass the right way this time," I said.

"What if I don't want you to love me?" She asked, propping her hand on her hip. "How do I know you've changed?"

"That fact that I haven't drug yo pigeon toed ass back to my house proves I've changed. But don't get shit fucked up, Nova, I will if I have to," I said. I stepped in her space. "And the kind of love you had for me don't die, so stop the bullshit."

She stared up at me trying to read me. This was the nigga whose heart she stole with her giving, kind, loving and goofy personality. I was finally the man that deserved her.

"Now come on, Maw and Paw cooked Van Camp pork n' beans and grits just for me," I said in an exaggerated country accent taking her hand. The giggle coming from her made my chest swell. I knew this didn't mean I stood a chance with her, but at least I didn't have to kidnap her again.

Nova stayed quiet the entire breakfast. She may've been shocked by my presence, but it didn't stop her greedy ass from eating the hell out of that turkey bacon her mom cooked. Me and Pops chose the fried pork chop. After breakfast was over, Pops took me out to the olive fields. I was amazed at the work he had done without any help from me. With Nova's help, he was in the progress of starting his own olive oil business. Me, still being a businessman, offered to invest with him. This time it wasn't about helping her parents. It was honestly a great investment.

After the tour, Pops told me to follow a path and I'd find Nova. He said she liked spending a lot of time alone by a small lake. I made my way down the path and found her coming out of the water dripping wet and naked. Nova was so comfortable in all her natural beauty she didn't shy away when she spotted me. She walked over to her towel that was laying on a small lounge chair.

"At least I know ain't nobody been hitting that," I joked. My treasure chest was hidden behind a bush of hair just like the texture on her head. She rolled her eyes at me.

"What if I told you that was a lie?" she asked boldly. "What if I said Dirk loved when I spilled my nectar all over his face and lap?"

She wanted to push me to react and I did. I wrapped my arm around her small waist and pulled her against my chest. Her body shuddered as she gasped for her breath. I stared down at her waiting for her to fight against the hold I had on her, but she didn't. She softened in my arm. I leaned down and gave her a peck on her lips. She pulled away from me.

"That nigga didn't even get a kiss," I said. "And you won't be hearing from him again."

"You killed him?" she asked shocked and sad.

I laughed. "Hell nah! He in jail for armed robbery. Yo ass out here dating criminals and shit. That's why you need me to protect you."

Nona Day   Over You

"I saw you with her," she said sadly.

"And only you would go out with a nigga after spilling smoothies all on him," I said smiling. Her mouth dropped open, because she had no idea I saw her. "She's a business partner and colleague. Even though I shitted on her wedding day, she looked out for me when shit was falling apart. She's ambitious and doing what needs to be done to place herself in a powerful position. It's business, nothing else," I said.

"Is she positioning herself on your lap?" she asked sarcastically.

"We can sit and talk about whatever you want to, but my dick hard as fuck right now. You gotta put on some clothes," I said. She giggled and wrapped the towel around her.

"Jarvis, I don't—" she started to speak before I interrupted her.

"Do you still love me, Nova?"

"You know I do, but it's not that simple," she said.

"Da fuck it ain't. You're the simplest person I know," I said. "I'm the reason shit was complicated."

She smiled at me. "You've found balance."

"Yea, so shut da fuck up and work with me on this shit," I said. "I gotta get going. I'm having a little party at *our* house tonight. It starts at nine o'clock. Don't be too late."

I turned to walk away but remembered she didn't have a car anymore.

"Bahka will be here at nine to pick you up," I said, not giving her the chance to decline. She could've easily taken her mother's car, but I wanted to make sure she came.

Later That Evening

I was coming out of the kitchen when I heard loud screaming. When I walked toward the foyer, I couldn't stop the smile that came across my face. Nova, Cache and Amoy were embracing like they hadn't seen each other in years. She looked beautiful as always. I actually liked the uncoordinated outfit she wore. Binx jumped out her arms and ran up the stairs. She gave me a warm smile as Amoy rushed out to the backyard where the gathering was being held.

Nova had a way with genuine people. Her energetic spirit spread kindness and love through everyone at that party. I sat back never taking my eyes off her as she interacted with everyone. This wasn't the normal stuffy people that she was used to meeting with me. These were acquaintances of mine that she'd never met.

"I told you that one was gon' be trouble for you," Dak said, sitting next to me by the pool. I chuckled and shook my head. In a few hours, Nova had everyone gathered in the backyard, that was lit up by outdoor lights, playing her favorite childhood games.

By the end of the night, I had no time with her. She was standing by the dessert table when I walked up behind her and whispered in her ear.

"Turn around and look up in the sky."

When she turned around the backyard lights went off. Amoy and Cache came out the sliding doors with an enormous birthday cake. Everyone started singing happy birthday to her as fireworks went off in the sky. The last set of fireworks spelled…Happy Birthday Nova.

Nona Day   Over You

"I know your birthday is over a week away, but I won't be here," I explained. "I'm going to Texas to spend a few days with some family." Amoy and I had reconnected with our Texas family and wanted to start spending more time with them.

Nova looked up at me with tears in her eyes. She walked into the house leaving me standing there. Amoy walked over to me.

"Go check on her," she said. "I got this."

I searched downstairs for her but couldn't find her. The last place I expected to find her was in our bedroom. She was sitting in her meditation area.

"This ain't the time for this shit, Nova," I said, walking over to her. I looked at Binx sitting on the bed. "Binx, get off the damn bed." Binx popped up and got off the bed.

"Sit down," she said, looking up at me. If this was what it took to get her back, I'd oblige. I sat on the floor across from her.

"Everything is still as I left it," she said.

"I couldn't bring myself to throw it away," I admitted. "It was like saying you was gone, and I wasn't ready to accept that."

"Do you know why I hated going to all those events and dinners with you?" she asked.

"At first, I didn't," I replied. "But now I understand. I was making you be someone you wasn't and that goes against everything that you are."

She looked surprised that I figured that out. I not only spent time working on myself. Some time was spent learning who Nova was without me.

"I don't wanna lose myself like that again," she said.

"I won't let you. And I won't ask you to be anything other than who you are," I promised her.

"Can we date and shit?" she asked. She still sounded weird as hell cussing.

I laughed. "Stop cussing, Nova."

She giggled. "That's the one bad habit I picked up from you that I like."

"We'll do that corny ass dating shit," I said. She smiled.

"I get to choose where and what we do for our first date," she said.

Three Days Later

Nova

*W*hen I opened the door to my she shed, I couldn't stop laughing. Jarvis stood at the door with his hands in oversized, orange, brown, black and yellow camo, cargo sweats, a purple graffiti styled T-shirt, and sandals. An orange beanie was on his head. Tears ran down my face as I fell on the bed with laughter. I didn't know why he was dressed like that, but it gave me a laugh for the day. His colorful outfit blended well with my orange skirt, purple and yellow top and white sneakers.

"Ain't shit funny, Nova," he said, stepping inside. "Now, where we going?"

"I'm not going anywhere with you dressed like that," I said, wiping the tears from my face as I sat up.

"Shit, this how you dress," he said seriously.

"I dress like this, because it's who I am. And I do not dress like that. My style is a fashion statement. You look like a darn fool," I said jokingly.

"Well we matching," he said. "I ain't going home to change."

I stood up in front of him.

"Are you serious?" I asked, smiling up at him.

"Yep, now come on," he said, turning to walk away.

I gently grabbed his arm. *The touch.* My hand on his flesh sent bolts of tingling sensations through my body. My flower started to blossom like a strong pulsing heart, causing me to bite on my bottom lip. He stepped close enough for me to taste his breath and placed his hand on side of my face. My mouth slightly opened wanting and waiting for what was in his eyes. Leaning down, he stroked his tongue across my bottom lip. My breathing became heavy.

"Pussy on fire right now, ain't it," he said with a smile. "Lil freaky ass."

"Butthole," I said lightly pushing him in the chest. He laughed. "I was going to tell you that you don't have to be like me to love me the right way. I love the charismatic, poised gentlemen as much as I love the rude, disrespectful side as long as you love both sides of you."

"Appreciate that," he said, tapping me on the butt. "But I wore these ugly ass clothes because I know you gon' have me doing some off the wall shit. So, I dressed the part."

I laughed.

Our first stop on our date was to a scrapbook expo. I had taken all the pictures from my phone that I had of us and printed them out at Walmart. We talked, laughed and enjoyed each other's company as we designed our scrapbook of love. Jarvis relished every minute of it and wanted to add some pictures from his phone. I refused to let him make a small personal scrapbook with the nudes he'd taken of me. I had several of him, but I was going to keep them locked in my phone.

The next stop was to a community event in one of his old stomping grounds. I thought he was going to be embarrassed to be seen in his outfit, but he had no shame. The way everyone reacted to seeing him, you would've thought he was an A-list celebrity. We sat on a small bench eating Hennessy flavored popcorn and ice cream.

"Damn, I forgot how much I miss this," he said looking around.

Nona Day   Over You

"I've started back volunteering with a lot of them," I said.

He looked at me with remorse in his eyes. "Sorry for taking you away from what you enjoyed doing."

I smiled, leaned over and kissed him on the cheeks.

"I enjoyed doing you too," I said. He chuckled. Nothing had changed between us. Our chemistry was undeniable.

Our date ended with paint balling and rock climbing. After an eventful day, Jarvis chose the restaurant. He was a regular customer at Bones Restaurant, so everyone looked at him like he had lost his mind when they saw his attire. Jarvis didn't seem bothered that he looked like a complete mess.

*****

He stood at my she shed door saying goodnight.

"So, what did you think of our date?" I asked smiling at him.

"I think yo ass got too much damn energy," he said. "I'm tired as fuck, but I had fun. A great time, Nova."

He leaned down and kissed me on the lips. Before I knew it, my back was pinned against the door swapping spit. I wanted every inch of his body. His hands caressed me, and I was ready to drop to my knees and swallow the hard package inside his pants. He broke our kiss pressing his forehead against mine.

"Goodnight wierdo," he said.

I giggled. "Goodnight stalker."

A Week Later

Jarvis and I talked every day on the phone, so the time we spent apart was obsolete. We would talk for hours about nothing. And more hours about things that mattered to us. He was still in Texas and I couldn't deny I was ready to see him again. When he brought me back into his life the first time, I wasn't sure of where we stood. This time I stayed positive and knew our love could overcome any obstacles. He seemed more willing to let me inside his deepest thoughts and I didn't shy away from letting him know what I wanted and needed from him to be happy in his life.

Nona Day   Over You

Tonight, I pulled Kendall out of the house to celebrate his second tea and coffee shop opening at the neo-soul lounge we had fallen in love with. Kendall knew where my heart was and nothing between us was awkward after his confession. He said I made it easy to still be my friend. I wasn't making the herbal blends anymore. My heart just wasn't into marketing and selling what I loved growing and producing, but I did still make them for his shops. It was the least I could do after what Jarvis did.

Jarvis had been calling my phone for the past hour. I kept ignoring his calls, because I didn't want him to know I was hanging with Kendall. We were in a good place and I didn't want to ruin it. As I was sitting at the bar waiting for Kendall to come out the bathroom, I felt eyes watching me. I scanned the room until my eyes landed on the entrance door. My heart plummeted to my feet. *Please God not again!* I sat still as a rock as he walked over to me.

"Why you ain't answering yo damn phone?" He said picking it up off the counter. I couldn't lie and say it was dead. He obviously saw it was on. My heartbeat pulsated through my entire body when I spotted Kendall walking in our direction. I wanted to scream for him to run in the other direction, but he marched his care-free behind in the lion's den.

Jarvis looked at Kendall as he stood beside me and back at me. I couldn't read the expression on Jarvis' face, but my mind was telling me to tell Kendall to run for his life. Kendall stood beside me like Jarvis didn't beat the crap out of him a few months ago.

"What up?" Kendall said to Jarvis with a head nod. I sat confused when they shook hands like nothing ever happened. Kendall looked at me.

"He came to see me a few weeks after shit happened and apologized. I wouldn't have accepted it, but he looked like he was going through enough as it was," Kendall informed me. "Plus he invested in my lil small ass beverage shop. Now I have two."

I looked at Jarvis in complete shock. His face was still void of any expression.

"Why didn't you tell me?" I asked both of them.

Kendall shrugged his shoulders. "He asked me not to tell you."

"Let's go," he said to me. He gave Kendall dap again and led me out of the lounge.

I climbed in the passenger seat of his Tesla. The ride to my parents' house was quiet and I didn't know how to feel about that. We'd talked nonstop when he was in Texas, now the only sound between us was Kevin Gates' *Love Bug*. It was obvious he wasn't mad about me hanging out with Kendall, so I didn't understand the bad vibe I was getting from him. When he pulled up to the house, I thought we would at least sit in the car and talk for a while. He quickly got out and came to my side and opened the door. Still not a word from him; he walked me to my little she shed, kissed me on the forehead and walked away. It wasn't a goodnight kiss. The kiss to my forehead was a goodbye. A cold chill went down my spine. It finally dawned on me.

"Jarvis, I'm sorry," I said still standing at the door. He ignored me and kept walking causing me to run after him. I caught up with him and grabbed his arm to stop him. "I said I was sorry."

He tilted his head, staring down at me. "For what, Nova."

"For avoiding your calls, because I was scared to let you know I was with Kendall. I thought you might get mad and do something stupid again," I confessed.

"You ain't ready for this shit, Nova," he said. "And I ain't with forcing it on you no more."

Now he pissed me off. I rushed up to him, standing in front of him. He stopped in his tracks.

"You forced me back into this the moment your overbearing behind knocked on my door! Now you gon' take the time to deal with me the same way I dealt with you," I said angrily. "Or God as my witness I will have you rooted up and slithering through the grass like a snake."

He stared at me to see just how serious I was.

"When I fuck you, I'm gon' fold yo lil ass up like a pretzel," he said seriously.

"Shut da fuck up and come inside." I said, grabbing his hand. "Besides I do yoga." He laughed.

He sat up on the bed with his back against the headboard watching television. I went into my small bathroom, got comfortable in an oversized T-shirt and sat beside him on the bed. Binx jumped up on the bed and into Jarvis' lap.

"When did this happen?" I asked.

"When you left us. We missed you so we bonded," he said.

"Thank you for doing that for Kendall," I said graciously.

"Ain't invest in his beverage shop for you, Nova," he said. "It was the least I could do, since he didn't press charges. I could've been sitting my ass behind bars."

I took Binx from his lap and put him out the door.

"So you gon' throw my damn cat out the door for snakes to eat him?" he asked. "You know damn well he's a city cat."

I laughed. "He has a kitty door at my parents' back door. Now get naked."

It was hilarious how fast he hopped out of the bed peeling his clothes off.

"Now sit back on the bed the same way you were sitting," I told him. He got comfortable with his hard rod lying on his muscular thigh. After removing my shirt, I walked over and straddled his lap. I hadn't planned on this happening, but I was glad I shaved yesterday. He closed his eyes and enjoyed the touch of our bodies against each other. My tongue stroked across his bottom lip. He reached up to touch me, but I stopped him by lacing his fingers between mine. He opened his eyes and gazed into mine. I moved my face close enough to his so our lips touched, and we were breathing into each other's mouths. His body started relaxing but I could feel his rod throbbing under my butt cheek. My hands caressed the contour of his face down to his muscular torso and arms. Jarvis was stuck in a trance of sensual, erotic passion. He took it as long as he could.

"Fuck Nova! Put my dick in you," he barked in agonizing ecstasy.

I smiled at him. "When I do promise me you won't come until I tell you to."

"Ain't promising no shit like that," he said. "For the past three months my dick only been in my hand. The first one gon' be fast and quick. I'll make it up to you."

I missed this part of him so much: blunt, honest and rude as hell. But I knew his love for me was pure.

"Well, we can't do this," I said, attempting to get up. He gripped my waist to stop me.

"Gah-damn! Fine! I won't come," he said. "Just put da mothafucka inside you."

I couldn't help but giggle.

"Keep your eyes on me," I told him.

Lifting off his lap, I reached down and held his throbbing member in my hand. He let out a low grunt as I massaged him. I placed his dome at my entrance and slowly slid down on him. Jarvis bit down on his bottom lip and his eyes rolled in the back of his head. Lacing his hands with mine again, I started winding my hips slowly. I could feel my wetness pouring on his rod. His heart was pounding inside my core. His breath started to become erratic as he fought the need to release. He closed his eyes tight trying to focus on not coming.

"Open up for me, Jarvis," I said still winding and grinding. He was deep inside me beating against my g-spot. "Don't focus on the sex. Look at me and ride this out with me."

He opened his eyes. Eyes that told me he wanted nothing but to love, protect and cherish me. We shared a love that was destined. I was so high off his love and energy I started to feel as if I was floating. When I felt my orgasm start to build, my slow winds turned into thrusting and gyrating. I was bucking and calling out his name.

"Fuck Nova!" He barked, unbinding our hands. Tears flowed down my face as he caressed my breasts with his hands and licked, sucked and nibbled on my nipples. I threw my head back and saw a galaxy full of beautiful bright stars. All that could be heard was the gushy wet sounds and our animalistic cries of pleasure. When I couldn't hold it any longer, I gripped his face between my hands, staring him in his eyes.

"Come with me," I said. A few more pumps and I spilled an ocean all over him. No sound came from Jarvis as he stared at me. I could feel his semen pouring into me. His eyes pleaded for understanding of what was happening. His face contorted as he kept unloading. His shaft was throbbing against my slippery walls as his cum continued to fill me up. When he finally finished, he jerked with a trembling leg. His eyes rolled back in his head. He looked as if he had took a hot shot in his main vein. I massaged his body to help bring him from the euphoric bliss. After a few minutes, he finally came down from his cosmic high. He slid down in the bed with me on top of him.

"Da fuck kinda sex was that?" he asked, still trying to catch his breath.

I giggled. "The best kind. So much for your pretzel style shit."

He smacked me on the ass. "Stop cussing."

"I love you."

"I love yo ass too, Nova," he said kissing the top of my head.

Two Weeks Later

Jarvis

$\mathcal{I}$ sat at my desk in my home office frustrated and stressed out. I'd been working my ass off trying to gain at least three more investors. My days of painting a facade to appease others was over, so the elite weren't feeling a nigga like me.

Nova's light snoring made me look up to see her stretched out on the office sofa. A few hours ago, she had me running around the house playing hide and seek. When I found her, I pinned her against the hall wall drilling my dick deep inside her. I could still feel the burning sensation from her clawing into my back. We were still trying to take things slow, but a day hadn't gone by without us spending time together. I hated to wake her up, but Valentine was coming over to discuss business. I walked over and stared down at her chocolate naked body causing my dick to wake up in my pajama pants.

Nona Day   Over You

"Nova," I said loud enough to wake her up. "Wake yo ass up and go get dressed."

"Where we going?" she asked, sitting up on the sofa.

"Nowhere. Valentine coming over to discuss some business," I told her.

She sat on the edge of the sofa and looked up at me with her sexy sleepy eyes. My dick jumped when she massaged it through my pajamas. I watched as she pulled it out and stroked her wet tongue over my dome. Her tongue teased and massaged my dick until precum seeped from my dome. Her freaky ass winked at me before sucking on my head like a lollipop. I started fucking her mouth and her throat opened for me.

"Damn I'm bout to bust this shit," I said as my toes started to curl up. She started moaning, sucking and devouring me until I yanked my dick from her mouth. "Bend over."

She turned around and bent over the couch with her ass in the air. I could smell the sweet aroma coming from her pussy. I dropped to my knees and sucked her pussy lips inside my mouth causing her to moan and dip her back. Her pretty chocolate pussy was right where I wanted it...in my face. I slid my tongue between her lips. She tasted so damn good. My tongue was twirling, stroking and dipping causing her to cry out my name. She started twirling her hips letting me know she was getting ready to come. I flicked my tongue on her swollen clit while sliding two fingers inside her. Her body shivered as she sprayed my entire mouth and face with her fluids. She twitched and whimpered as she tried to ride the wave out, but I didn't give her time. I drilled my dick deep making her pussy cream as her walls locked down on me.

"Gah-damn I love fuckin' you," I groaned as I started thrusting in and out of her. I gripped a handful of her hair and pulled her back against my chest. My free hand slid between her soaked pussy lips and started massaging her clit.

"Aaaaahhh yeeesss," she cried out. She wrapped her hand around me and pulled my face down to hers. Our lips locked and she sucked my tongue inside her mouth while her pussy sucked my dick in deeper. Our animalistic fucking instantly turned into some deep passionate love making. That was the kind of shit Nova did to me. She took me to a place that made my insides turn to mush. She broke our kiss.

Nona Day   Over You

"I love you so much," she said against my lips as I slid in and out of her in slow motion. I was so far gone; getting over her was a damn joke. I could never find the words at moments like this. She took me to a place inside of her that always left me speechless. I felt myself getting ready to explode. Wrapping my arms around her waist, I started pounding inside her until we exploded together.

I scooped her up in my arms, carried her upstairs and laid her across the bed. I took a shower to get ready for the meeting with Valentine.

Thirty minutes later, Valentine walked into my home office. She had a list of possible investors she wanted to look over. I was hoping I could at least get three from the list. I wanted a total of eight investors, but I'd settle for six. Dak, Noble and I had agreed to put in more than what we intended. We weren't scared to take the gamble, but we wanted investors that vibed with us. There wouldn't be drug money in our bank, but it would be used to bank drug money that had been washed.

She took a seat in front of my desk smiling at me.

"What's the smile for?" I asked.

"You're glowing. I guess the gypsy makes you happy," she said. I laughed. Everyone had a story about who Nova was because we didn't bother to explain who she was to anyone. The only people that needed to know were Nova and me.

"Where's the list?" I asked. She reached in her briefcase and pulled out a piece of paper. I took it and scanned the names. Not one damn name on the list was worth my time. Everyone on the list was squeaky clean. I needed investors with a little dirt on their name.

Nova peeped in the room and I gestured for her to come in.

"I'm sorry to interrupt. I just wanted to let you know I'm going home," she said standing nervously at the door. I couldn't stop the scowl from appearing on my face. Valentine looked over her shoulder at Nova.

"Hi," Nova said waving at her, forcing a smile. Valentine threw her hand up and turned back around.

I stood up and walked over to Nova. Something was off with her, but I couldn't figure it out. She seemed nervous and scared. After everything we'd been through, I knew she wasn't tripping about me working with Valentine.

"Come here, Valentine," I said standing in front of Nova, staring down at her. Valentine walked over and stood next to me.

"You don't have to like her, but you will respect her as the woman I love," I said with my eyes still on Nova. "Nova, ain't shit between me and Valentine but business, so I would appreciate it if you respected her on that level."

"Fine with me as long as she knows her place," Nova said looking at Valentine.

"Trust me, I do," Valentine said. "I'm not emotionally or sexually interested in Jarvis…anymore. My only concern is to see him and myself succeed."

"I want that too," Nova said to her.

"Well, we on the same team," Valentine said winking her eye at Nova. A half smile spread across Nova's face.

"Just don't be coming up in here thinking you run shit," Nova said jokingly. "I'll hate to have to show you my kung fu moves." Nova started imitated kung fu kicks and jabs making all of us laugh.

"Duly noted," Valentine replied with a smile.

"Give me a minute," I said to Valentine. She walked back over and sat in the office chair.

"This is yo damn home, Nova," I said looking down at her. "It's time to put this 'taking it slow' to rest. Now sit down. We'll talk after this meeting."

She walked over and sat on the sofa. By the end of the meeting, Valentine wasn't happy with the investors I chose, but it wasn't her bank. If she wanted to lead the legal team, she needed to vet the ones I chose and be quiet.

Nova had slipped out of the office on me. If she left, this time I was dragging her ass back home by that wooly hair of hers. Lucky for her, I found her sitting at the kitchen isle eating fruit. I walked over and sat next to her.

"Why you ain't ready to move back in?" I asked.

She looked at me. "It still amazes me how you go from this to what I seen in your office."

"Gah-damn, Nova! I'm still me," I said angrily. "I'm balancing the shit. I like being that nigga you saw in my office when I have to be. Being him wasn't my problem. The problem was I thought no one wanted this me. I've learned not to give a damn about what they wanted," I said pointing at myself. "Now you gon' start tripping?"

"Why you doing all that?" she asked smiling at me. "All I said was I was amazed by it. You being very dramatic right now, Jarvis."

She sat there with a goofy ass smile on her face.

"Well you should've worded it different," I said calming down. She leaned over and kissed me on the jaw. "Now, what's up with you?"

She shrugged her shoulders. "Does it bother you that I'm not motivated the way Valentine is. She's ambitious, beautiful and smart. I'm just Nova."

"You simple as fuck, weird as hell, no sense of fashion but your pure soul is magnetic, and let's not get started on yo pussy game," I said seriously. She laughed and nudged my shoulder.

"I still have all my things at my apartment in Dothan," she said.

"No you don't. I bought the building and moved everything out," I told her. I knew I wasn't letting her go back to Dothan the moment I slid inside her.

SOUL Publications

"Jarvis!" She yelped. I pulled her chair closer to me and started kissing on her neck.

"You gon' move back in?" I asked. She giggled.

"Can I think about it overnight?" she asked. "I want to pray on this…alone. I'm going to stay at the she shed tonight."

I didn't like it, but I understood, therefore I didn't argue with her about it.

"So you ain't gon' sell yo herbs and oils anymore?" I asked.

"It's just not anything I'm passionate about, so it feels like too much work," she said. "I mean I don't mind hard work. I just wanna do something I'm passionate about. My love is growing the herbs and making the oils but not to sell them. I actually know what I want to do."

"What?" I asked curiously.

"I know you'll probably laugh but I've really been thinking about it," she said. "I want to open a farming school. I've been researching grants and loans that I can apply for to get started. There's plenty of land for sale near my parents which would be a great location."

I smiled at her.

"Don't laugh, Jarvis," she said rolling her eyes at me. "I know it won't make me millions of dollars or probably any money, but it's what I love doing. A lot of people are getting into growing their own produce. I have a green thumb to help show them how. I've always wanted to do something to help others and this is what I love doing."

"I ain't laughing," I said. "I think it's dope as hell and so are you. I'll match whatever is raised by the fundraisers we bout to start having for you. So, I suggest you put that master's degree to work and start drawing up plans and shit for this school."

She threw her arms around my neck and hugged me tight.

Nova

I sat by the lake on my father's farm. Every few seconds I would stare out at the water and then back at my hand. I was so caught up into him coming back into my life that I didn't think. I didn't think about how I stopped taking the pill to cleanse my body during our breakup. Now I was sitting here looking at a positive pregnancy test. My body had been so drained the past week, but I thought it was because of all the sex we were having. There hadn't been any morning sickness to prompt my suspicions; it was only a feeling in my gut. After I left his house, I rushed to the drug store and grabbed three tests. All tested positive. I had to be approximately a month late.

It happened the night we made love in my she shed. I was so scared he wasn't going to be happy about our baby. He was trying to accomplish his biggest goal yet. The last thing he needed was more responsibility. He wanted me to move in, but I wasn't sure how he would feel about *us* moving in. I had sent him a text this morning to come to my parents' house. A couple of hours had passed, and I was getting impatient. Just when I was getting ready to go back to my parents' house, he came walking down the path in a suit. He walked over, took off his jacket, loosened his tie, removed his shoes, and sat with his legs crossed like me.

"Yo father liked to talk me to damn death," he said. I laughed. "Sorry it took me awhile getting here. I was caught up in a meeting. What's up?"

It must've been the hormones because I became overly sensitive as my eyes started to water.

"I'm pregnant," I said. I dropped my head, but I could feel his eyes on me.

"Thought you was on the pill or something?" he asked.

"I was but when we broke up, I went through a spiritual cleansing," I told him. "I stopped taking the birth control."

"How far along are you?" he asked.

"At least a month," I answered. "I think it happened the night in my she shed."

"You mean the night we had the voodoo sex?" he asked. I couldn't tell if he was joking or serious, because his facial expression held no humor. "So, you carrying a voodoo doll?"

I stared at him to see if he was serious. He held a straight face for about a minute. It was a relief to see his lips curl up into a smile.

"You're not mad?" I asked.

"Da fuck I'm gon' be made about my wife carrying my seed for?" he asked.

"You have so much going on. I just didn't know how you would feel about adding more to your plate," I said.

"Nova, it ain't shit that comes before you, and now our child," he said.

"You called me your wife," I said smiling at him.

"Yea, you better not had sold that damn ring," he said seriously.

"I'll be back," I said, jumping up.

I rushed back to my she shed and retrieved the ring from the small box under my bed. When he left the beautiful ring on the dresser, my heart melted. It wasn't an exquisite, fancy ring. It was a simple, beautiful princess cut diamond. The diamond was huge but not too fancy. It was perfect for me. I rushed back to see him smoking a blunt. Taking my seat across from him, I placed the ring on the blanket between us.

"Ask me again," I said smiling at him.

"I ain't never ask yo ass to marry me," he said.

"Oh," I said, dropping my head. I felt like such an idiot. Here I was thinking he wanted me to be his wife for real. He lifted my chin forcing me to look at him.

"I didn't think I had to ask you because our hearts and souls were already married," he said, smiling at me.

I smiled, threw my arms around him and covered his face with kisses.

"Yes, I'll marry you," I said between kisses. He laughed.

"Now, we gotta consummate the engagement by fucking in the lake," he said. "Kinda like a baptism engagement."

It was my turn to laugh.

"No, we have to promise each other," I said. "I'm going to promise you something that I'll do as your wife. You'll promise me something as my husband."

"You so damn dorky," he said laughing. "I ain't never heard of no shit like that."

"So, it's what I want to do," I said smiling. "This is just us, the Gods and universe. No rehearsal or show for everyone else."

"Man, you be having me doing some corny mess," he said, shaking his head.

"Just reciprocate my promises with yours," I said, taking his hands into mine. "First we pray."

I closed my eyes for a few seconds and peeped to see if he was following my lead. I smiled when I saw his eyes closed. We prayed silently.

"Go ahead," he said, nodding his head. I reached over and held both of his hands in mine.

"I promise to bring you peace," I said to start.

"I promise to give you happiness, Nova," he said. He was taking this as serious as I was. This man loved me as much as I loved him.

"I promise to stimulate you," I replied.

"I promise to encourage you," he said, winking at me.

Nona Day   Over You

"I promise to stand by you through good and bad," I promised.

"I promise to lead you with love and respect," he said.

"I promise to listen and be understanding," I said knowing we still had more to learn from each other.

"I promise to be open with you," he said. I knew he meant those words. He had changed a lot during our breakup.

"I promise to love you infinitely," I said feeling myself getting teary eyed.

"I promise to cherish your love," he vowed, holding my hands tighter.

"I love you, Jarvis Michael Alexandria."

"Yea I love yo corny ass too, Nova Lee Champagne."

I leaned forward for a deep, sensual, wet, sloppy kiss. We sat and talked for hours before the sun started to set. I followed him back to our house in my car. Binx rode shotgun with him.

When we got home, and I followed him upstairs to our bedroom. He sat on side of the bed. I took a long shower and walked out into the bedroom and smelled sage. Jarvis was relaxed on the bed with his back against the headboard smoking. The laughter that roared from me echoed through the bedroom.

"What da hell so funny?" he asked.

"You're smoking sage leaves," I said with laughter.

He looked at the blunt.

"I was wondering where you got this weak ass shit!" he said, putting the sage filled blunt out. "Why you got it rolled up like a blunt?"

"I was bored and high as hell one night while you was sleeping, so I crumbled up the few leaves and rolled them up. I figured I could place them throughout the house and burn them when needed," I told him.

He chuckled and shook his head. "Only you, Nova."

He opened the nightstand and pulled out the liquid marijuana I had made. I went to the dresser to slip on something comfortable.

"I moved all yo clothes to the next bedroom. You junky as hell, Nova," he said. "I like my things neat and organized."

He was right, so I didn't have a problem with that. We had too many clothes for the enormous closet in the master bedroom. In the next bedroom, I slid the closet door open. All the expensive name brand clothes were hanging tidily on one side. On the other side, all of my clothes I had left in Dothan hung neatly also. My crazy shoe game were stacked along with the boring shoes Sandy picked out for me.

Jarvis walked up behind me wrapping his arms around my waist.

"I give it a week before this closet looks like a damn tornado been through it," he said. I laughed because he was right.

I turned around to face him with a smile.

"Thank you."

"You're welcome," he said. "Now, get dressed. We gotta date night in the backyard."

Our night was spent talking, laughing, eating smores and watching *Frozen*. We made a pact to not drink or smoke until the baby was born. I wanted to breast feed, so he only agreed to the pact during the pregnancy. I was on my own after that. We attempted to watch the movie, but I fell asleep in his arms.

One Month Later

A couple of weeks ago, we staged a big performance for family and friends at the house. Jarvis dropped to one knee and asked me to be his wife. As far as we were concerned, we were already married. The proposal, engagement and wedding would be for everyone else and the legal papers. I couldn't hide my pregnancy from Amoy and Cache for more than a week. They knew I smoked like a chimney, so it didn't take them long to figure out why I wasn't drinking or smoking. Mama cried like a baby seeing her daughter getting engaged. Daddy stood tall like a proud, happy father.

I was looking in the closet for an outfit to wear. Jarvis was having a dinner party for all the investors and their wives tonight. This meant so much to him and I didn't want to mess it up. He told me to wear what I wanted to, but I wasn't sure how I wanted to present myself as his fiancée. As I contemplated on what to wear I truly understood what Jarvis was going through. Regardless of how he dressed or carried himself, he had to front to satisfy others. Now, he was able to be himself because he didn't give a damn who did or didn't like him. He had forgiven himself and healed from all the hurt and regret he felt.

I wanted to wear something classy and sophisticated but still be me. Jarvis was yelling from downstairs telling me to hurry and get dressed, because guests would be arriving soon. I took a deep breath and picked out my outfit. Twenty minutes later, I was walking down the stairs toward my fiancé. Like always, he didn't seem impressed by my blue and white polka dot vintage 50s dress. My hair was pinned up into a neat bun and a pair of black stilettos covered my feet.

"If you don't like it, I can change," I said nervously, stepping off the last step.

"You like it?" he asked. I nodded my head with a smile. "Then we good and I actually do love it."

The first guests to arrive were Amoy and Dak followed by Cache and Noble. Fifteen minutes later, Rochelle escorted the other guests into the den where we were having cocktails. The three men were tall, dark and handsome and their wives were absolutely gorgeous. When Jarvis called me over to introduce me, I became nervous. I hoped they weren't the type of acquaintances I was used to meeting of his.

"Everyone this the voodoo witch y'all done heard about, Nova," Jar said jokingly. I giggled and nudged him in the side. They all laughed. "Nova, this is King and his wife Jiera. The mean looking nigga is Vicious and his wife, Dove. Last but not least is future mayor and governor, Frost and his wife, Bubbles."

"Nigga, you can't be introducing us like that," Frost said jokingly to Jarvis. "My name is Frederick. The mean looking one's name is Victor."

I didn't feel the pressure to act a certain way or get any bad vibes from them. The ladies immediately complimented me on my unique style, and it felt genuine. Everyone started making small talk and sipping on some of my wine. It wasn't long before we were called into the banquet room for dinner. As hosts of the dinner party, Jarvis sat on one end of the table while I sat on the other end. I missed his hand being between my thighs. We all chatted effortlessly about any and everything. These men were professional, distinguished gentlemen but had a hard exterior that couldn't go unnoticed by the elite. These were the men that convinced Cornell Singleton to agree to become chairman of the bank. Here Jarvis was thinking he wanted elite privileged type investors. All he wanted was the type of men he saw in Jarvis..

"So Nova, I know you're not a witch, but why do the blogs think you are?" Jiera asked.

"I practice spirituality. A lot of close-minded people thinks it's witchcraft, spells and roots, or whatever they wanna call it," I said. "Spirituality is no different from religion. Everyone tries to walk in the path of their Higher Power. We're no different. We just strive to achieve the highest power within ourselves. Our God lives in us."

"That's dope," Bubbles said nodding her head.

"I get that," Dove said. "We all know what it takes to be a giving, loving, compassionate, forgiving, and honest person. That's something with strive for every day within us."

"Exactly," I said.

I looked across the table to see Jarvis staring at me. The look in his eyes told me he was taking me to the moon tonight. He lips slowly curled up and he winked his eye at me.

Epilogue

Four Months Later

*J*arvis had everything he needed to start his own bank: investors, board members, licenses and whatever else he needed. The foundation for the new building would start being laid in a week. I decided to make my farming school privately owned, because I didn't want the government telling me what I could and couldn't do. As soon as I brought our baby into our lives, I planned to start building on the land Jarvis purchased for me. He also started an engineering scholarship in Brandon's name along with a few other scholarships.

"My baby girl getting married," Daddy said standing beside me. Today I was promising myself to my soulmate in front of family and friends. Daddy and I stood together facing the closed double doors of the Miami beach house. Jarvis purchased the beach house with the swinging bed and honored my wish to be married on a beach. On the other side of the door was the man that I couldn't forget, the man that I couldn't get over. My soulmate that was

344

Nona Day   Over You

inside of me spiritually, mentally, and emotionally. Our energies were so connected and powerful.

When the doors opened, I saw everyone standing. Jarvis stood under an ivory flowered arch waiting for me. The patio was so close to the beach Daddy and I didn't have far to walk. My five-month belly wasn't very big, but it was visible under my ivory, lace dress. Everyone smiled and Ma cried as Daddy placed my hand in Jarvis' hand. Jarvis and I had already said our vows to each other at the lake, so we did the traditional exchanging of vows for everyone. Jarvis stared at me with so much love in his eyes all I could do was let my tears slide down my face.

"If anyone can show just cause why this couple cannot lawfully be joined together in matrimony, let them speak now or forever hold their peace," the pastor said. No one spoke, but when Jarvis started speaking my heart started to pound. He stared at me with the nonchalant demeanor I was too familiar with. This was the facial expression that didn't give a damn.

"Yea, I got something to say," Jarvis said, never looking away from me. I could feel myself getting lightheaded.

"What are you doing?" I heard Amoy asked in a loud whisper, standing behind me.

"Nova, we promised to always be open and honest with each other, right?" he asked. All I could do was nod because the lump in my throat wouldn't let me talk. Hell, I could barely breathe. "I have to tell you that you are beautiful regardless of what you have on, but that's an ugly ass wedding dress. I mean I gave you a blank check, Nova."

If I wasn't so relieved, I would've been furious with him. Amoy and Cache snickered from behind me. Over Jar's shoulder, Dak and Noble chuckled and shook their heads.

"You're an asshole," I said smiling at me.

"You love me though," he said, smiling and winking at me. "Go ahead, Rev."

Four Months Later

Jarvis and I sat in our huge tub with my back against his chest. It took a lot to convince him to let me have a water birth, but he finally agreed. The midwife was in the bathroom with us to monitor everything. Jarvis wanted to know the gender, but I wanted it to be a surprise. This baby kicked inside of me the entire pregnancy and now it was whooping my behind to get out. My body tensed up when I felt another contraction coming. I squeezed Jarvis' hand and tried my hardest not to cry out in pain.

"Nova, we need to go to a damn hospital," he said. "You in too much pain."

I didn't reply until I felt relief from the contraction.

"I'll be in the same pain at the hospital, Jarvis," I told him. "Nurse Kay is qualified to handle everything if something goes wrong."

"She gah-damn sho better be or her ass is dead if shit don't go right," he said. She smiled at him, but she didn't know how serious he was.

I leaned my head back so I could see his face.

"I need you to help me relax. Put all your energy into positive thoughts. Think about how great of a dad you're going to be, and us raising this baby that we created with love," I told him.

"How many we having?" he asked.

"As many as you want," I said. I didn't have any siblings, so I wanted a big family. Our house was big enough to have as many as my body would push out. I talked about names and things we'd be doing with our baby to calm him down. His body started to relax as he held me.

A couple of hours later, I pushed out a beautiful, eight-pound-four-ounce baby boy. Of course he was named after his father. I was exhausted but nothing could stop me from holding our love in my arms. I looked back at Jarvis to see a tear slide down his face as he stared at our son in my arms. Our love had created perfection to join us in our own little world.

The End

CPSIA information can be obtained
at www.ICGtesting.com
Printed in the USA
LVHW011704200820
663740LV00006B/949